Rest Area 10

Ron Freeman

ISBN 978-1-63844-151-9 (paperback)
ISBN 978-1-63844-152-6 (digital)

Christian Faith Publishing, Inc.
832 Park Avenue
Meadville, PA 16335
www.christianfaithpublishing.com

Printed in the United States of America

Chapter 1

It was a quiet evening. William was enjoying a hot cup of tea after a long day at the hospital.

After more than forty years as an ER doctor, he had finally learned how to relax at home and put his day's activities in proper perspective. He had built a fire in the fireplace and was simply beginning a relaxing evening in his den. It was his escape from all the complexities of a life in modern medicine, where everyone wanted a quick solution to all of their problems they were experiencing. Most patients lacked the desire to really understand why they had their problems. No one wanted to admit that what they were experiencing was oftentimes due simply to their own misplaced actions in poor judgment.

Good health, as William had learned, was more of a result of decisions based on correct eating habits coupled with proper exercise. But who wanted this type of remedy? Solutions to most were simply based on what pill to take. But William clearly understood that this type of medicine was based solely on symptom resolution and not problem identification and eradication.

He relaxed in his chair, sighed, and, as always, thought of the past and what and how he had learned all that really mattered to him. He thought of a young girl, critically ill and how she was treated, and quietly wondered what had ever happened to her.

Interrupting his thoughts, the doorbell rang. He rose from his chair, walked to the door, and opened it, finding a young woman, possibly in her thirties.

He smiled. "Can I help you?"

She smiled. "I am sorry for interrupting your evening, but are you Dr. William Scott?"

He looked at her. "My friends call me William." He stuck his hand out to shake hers. "How can I help you?"

She relaxed her grip on his firm handshake. "I'm sorry for coming to you unannounced, but I have driven a long way just to find some answers."

"Answers about what?" He motioned to her. "Come in, please."

He led her to the den and the warm fire.

He motioned to her. "Please sit, and tell me why you're here."

Just then a lady came into the den.

William looked up. "This is my wife, Maria."

Maria smiled at the young woman. "And you are?"

Somewhat embarrassed, the young woman looked at both William and Maria. "I'm sorry. I am Kelly Brown."

Maria looked at William with subdued intensity. William met her gaze with the same intensity.

Memories are never far away when they come from Rest Area 10. Both knew very well who this young woman was. They did not know her story past her involvement in Rest Area 10 but knew that it would be forthcoming.

Maria said, "Well, I'm glad to meet you, Kelly. Would you like a cup of tea?"

William noticed her hesitation. "Please have a cup of tea with me."

Maria left the den to get another cup of tea.

William looked at Kelly. "Now tell me what has brought you here."

Kelly thought for a second. What she had heard about William from her father surely had to be all true. He was a kind, compassionate man whose speech had a soothing effect on her. She looked at him, then the fire, and began.

"Not long ago my father died, a year or so after my mother. A day or so before he did, he told me an unbelievable story that he said happened near here and involved you as a young doctor. I'm simply searching for the truth and answers."

Maria came back in with Kelly's tea and handed it to her. "Enjoy." She smiled and left the den.

Kelly relaxed and took a drink of tea. "You may think I'm off base with what I'm about to say, but this is what my father told me as he was dying."

William's mind flashed to the past of many years ago. He looked at Kelly expectantly.

She looked at him with a surprised expression on her face and with a tear in her eye. "It's true, isn't it? There is a Rest Area 10, isn't there? It did happen, didn't it?"

William thought of what had happened and how it had opened his eyes to the possibilities that do exist. He looked at her, thought for a second, then slowly and softly began, "This may take a while."

She smiled at him. "That's fine. That's why I am here."

"What your father told you is probably all true. It did happen, and yes, there is a Rest Area 10. Maybe not as most would understand, but it does exist for those that need it. Before I tell you about that, however, I want to tell you something of me first. It may give you some insight into the whole experience of Rest Area 10. Rest Area 10 not only changed the lives of those that were fortunate to stop there, but it significantly altered my whole philosophy on my own life and why I was doing what I was. It affected me as a doctor and as a person.

"I really didn't know what my life as a doctor would be like. I had all these indications and dreams of what I had hoped to obtain through a life in medicine. I guess I was first led to medicine because I had dreamed of helping people. That's how I had grown up. That's how my parents had taught me. I really wanted to improve people's lives somehow. I was dedicated in thought and theory to a life spent helping others, but somehow, I got lost along the way. Maybe materialism contributed to that, the need to acquire what everyone else had. You know—big house, big cars, and fancy far-off vacations. And I had all that. I had everything that I could ever want.

"And I think I would have been satisfied had I not been introduced to a side of life that most never see. In fact, many don't know it may even exist. It's a world where possibilities are endless, where your only limitation are your own insecure thoughts of what may or may not be necessary to sustain life. I learned that knowledge may or may not exist in an institution. I learned that the greatest contributions to this world, to our lives, exist just out of eyesight and they may come to us from the most unlikely of sources.

"A very small insignificant piece of land led me on a learning experience that I had not expected and due to conventional medicine, it was difficult to grasp or even comprehend. But as I moved along on this journey, I began to realize that my confidence must and can only be found in a power far greater than anything I had ever learned in med school.

"This was something I was not looking for. It was something that I stumbled into or, more honestly, found me. It came to me as a surprise. An explosion of thoughts and questioning ideas that met me as I was unaware of its approach. Had it been stalking me? Was it waiting for me? Was it waiting for the proper time to appear? Yes, I believe it was waiting for a time when my intellect could grasp its full meaning. I was once again a student, about to be taught by the greatest Teacher I had ever known.

"In the back of our minds, as doctors, we know we can only do so much to help human life, to sustain it through normally occurring problems. But when those become too much for our abilities to deal with, overcome, or even comprehend, where do we turn? What recourse is there? What avenue do we look down or search for? Or do we simply allow the problems of the living to consume and destroy life? Do we insulate ourselves so far away from life's eventualities that we gradually lose the caring that is necessary to look further, to look deeper into finding solutions that may exist outside of our realm of understanding or our abilities?

"Maybe I came to a crossroads, a point of decision-making where there were more questions than answers, a point where I realized that hope could not be found in what I knew but in what I did not know, in what I did not understand. At this point in my professional life, all things began to change. I began finding answers to problems that I, as a doctor, did not even know existed. And it began with one sick child and a very caring set of parents. Through their situation and the explanation of what had happened to them, my understanding and attitude regarding the whole process of healing changed dramatically through their specific experience and similar ones that I was directly involved in. I began to slowly learn that I could be more than simply an ER doctor. I learned I was a servant, a man no greater or less than those I was attempting to heal. I learned that there is One who possesses more knowledge and healing power than all the doctors combined. And all He uses are kind words and soft touches. And finally, I learned there is a God and He does walk among us."

William looked at the fire, then back to Kelly. He smiled at her and continued, "You were the little girl whose parents were so fortunate to stop in Rest Area 10. We may never know why that happened, or even why He chose you and your family."

Kelly interrupted him. "Do you believe that the maintenance worker was really God?"

"Yes, there is no doubt in my mind because over many years that same scenario has played out many times involving different people suffering from different problems. Each encounter that I knew about involved one person or two, and each time a worker from the rest area offered something of value to the person or persons needing help. At times, the person would be healed of whatever their affliction was, or maybe the worker simply gave the person a new direction to take in their life or just simply kind words or a reassuring touch. But always something happened that placed the person in a better frame of mind or physical state."

William looked from the fire, from the past to the present to Kelly. She had tears in her eyes.

He continued, "Like I told you, I began to realize there was so much more to life and the healing of the living than I as a doctor was even aware of. It began to take hold of me. He began to take hold of me and the power that He gave me, or I should say that the power He shared with me was without limits. It was without scope in human terms." He paused, looked from Kelly to the fire, then back to her. "The more I was aware of His power in my life, the greater my abilities as a doctor became. I could not cure all of my patients, but through Him, I could heal them from what life had given them.

It didn't matter who was at fault. It only mattered who was now in charge of their lives."

Tearfully, Kelly responded, "My father told me I needed to somehow find you. That there was much more to the story of Rest Area 10 than even he comprehended. He wasn't sure about it, but because of what had happened to us, he knew there had to be more. Has it ever changed? Have the occurrences ceased?"

William sat back in his recliner, sighed deeply, and smiled. "No, they have not. And prayerfully, they will continue long after we are gone."

Maria came back into the den. "Will you be joining us for dinner, Kelly?"

"Oh, I can't."

"But you must," said William. "We have a lot more to discuss, and I truly believe that's why you're here. You see, we did not know when you would come, but we did know you would come." He looked deeply into her, into his own questioning thoughts and continued, "You see, Kelly, the reach of Rest Area 10 in your life will never cease either. Its influence will follow you. He will follow you. It will never end. Since that time as a small child in that rest area, He has never not been with you."

Kelly looked at William as warm tears filled her eyes. "That is one reason why I had to find you. I knew if what my father told was true, I had to hear more. I had to hear your thoughts and how it has affected your life, not only as a person but also a doctor. You see, I became a doctor. And I needed to know how those events have changed your perspective as a doctor."

Chapter 2

William looked at Kelly with understanding eyes and began. "When your parents brought you into our ER because of recommendations from the hospital you were first at, we had anticipated a very sick child. We were led to believe you were critical, and I'm sure the attending physician in the first hospital thought you were. In fact, your parents didn't wait for an ambulance. They put you back in their car and raced here, but on their way here, you became thirsty and they stopped in a rest area to possibly get you something to drink. But all they found was a maintenance worker with no vending machines for something to drink. He helped them by getting water out of an old-style well with a manual hand pump on it. He told your parents that he called it his living water. He gave you a drink of it, touched your head, and gave some encouraging words to your parents. He then sent you and your parents on your way here. But when you arrived at our ER, you appeared to be much better.

"And when we asked about what had occurred between both hospitals, all your parents told us was that you had stopped in a rest area. I asked where this rest area was located. When your father told us, we both looked at them in a way they noticed something was amiss. Your father asked me if there was something wrong. I told him that neither he nor his wife might believe what I was about to say.

I explained there is no rest area in that location, but that for those lucky enough to have a need, it does exist.

"At that moment, your mother had a very strange look on her face and immediately started crying. Your father looked at her and said, 'What is it, Nicky?' She looked at all of us and, through tears streaming down her face, told us that when the worker gave you a drink of water, he called you by name. Your mom wiped her tears and continued, saying they never told the worker your name. She tried to say something further but couldn't. Her emotions took over at that point.

"After a short discussion to soothe your parents, we admitted you for overnight observation, and your mother stayed with you. Wanting to know more, I took your father out for coffee, and he related the complete story to me. He told me about the rest area, that it was just around a curve on Highway 61. He told me he wanted to drive out there the next day when he got up and asked if I would like to go along. I told him I would very much like to go."

"Did you go?"

"Yes. We got up early and drove to that location, but as I suspected, no rest area. We stopped just after the curve, pulled over, and got out of the car to walk around the side of the road."

"Did you find anything? What happened?"

"Your father stopped, bent down, and picked something up. I asked him, 'What is it?' He turned to me. His face was white, and he stared at me, holding a small metal cup. He said, 'This is the exact cup the worker gave Kelly a drink out of.' 'Are you sure?' He stared at it in disbelief and began to cry. 'Yes, it's the cup. I could never forget it because it has a Cross scratched on the side.' He showed the cup to me and the Cross. I asked if I could hold it. He handed it to me, and when I took hold of it, I immediately got a mental picture of the maintenance worker. It was very powerful and very moving. I will never forget it."

William pointed to the mantle above the fireplace.

There in the middle of the long wooden mantel rested a small metal cup, and on the side of the cup was scratched a Cross.

A chill ran through Kelly, and the hair stood up on the back of her neck. She was speechless.

William looked at her. "You may hold it if you want."

"I would very much like that."

He got out of his chair, walked to the fireplace, retrieved the cup, and handed it to Kelly.

Before taking it, she asked, "Do you think something may happen if I touch it?"

"I can't answer that," he said, "but I hope it does."

He placed the small cup in her open hands. Their eyes met, and for a moment in time, all life stopped. In that moment as both hands still touched the cup, the earth moved. In their minds, the past became the present and pictures surrounding Rest Area 10 filled their thoughts. It only lasted a few seconds, but those few seconds in time would have a lasting effect on Kelly.

Tears streamed down her face as she handed the cup back to William.

"The cup is yours now. It's a reminder of what happened and what can happen and Who is really in charge of our lives."

"Oh, I can't. It's yours."

"No, I was simply keeping it safe for you. It has always been yours."

Maria came into the den and handed a Kleenex to Kelly. "Supper is ready." She motioned. "This way."

Chapter 3

They left the den and walked into a dining area where the table was set.

William looked at Kelly. "Please sit."

Kelly sat on one side of the wooden table across from Maria while William sat at the end.

"I hope you like soup and salad. William and I are light eaters."

"Oh, yes. It looks wonderful."

Kelly looked at William.

He bowed his head. "Let's pray. Father, thank You for our food and all the hands that placed it before us. And thank You also for the discussion we are about to have." He looked at both women. "Please eat."

Kelly began with her soup, but as she did, she kept looking at the table. She looked at William. "This table is gorgeous. Where did you get it?"

William smiled at her. "I made it."

"Where did you learn how to build something like this?"

William looked at her, then Maria. "Oh, I have known this old carpenter for many years. He gave me lots of help. He has always been a very good teacher."

She smiled and looked at Maria. "Oh, I see." She thought a little more and laughed quietly. "Oh, I really do see. You have great insight into Him, don't you?"

Maria looked at her and then to William and back to Kelly. "Over the years, with all of the occurrences that came to us in the ER, William learned to really listen to the thoughts that floated to him from our Lord. We never began a day in the ER without recognizing where our abilities and talents come from."

"You're a doctor also then?"

"Yes, we have worked side by side for many years."

Maria looked at William. "Did you tell her?"

"Tell me what?"

"Go ahead. You can tell her," said William.

"On our way here to assume our new positions as ER doctors, we also encountered Rest Area 10. At the time, it all seemed very normal, but it didn't take long for us to realize that Rest Area 10 only existed for those that needed it, and lucky for William and me, we were two that needed it."

"This is just all so amazing to me. I would assume there are many more stories like mine," said Kelly.

William looked at Kelly. "There are many, and we will share them with you. You need to understand what has happened here because here is where you will next practice."

Kelly looked surprised at William's revelation. She had a good job, she thought, but maybe William knew something she didn't.

He noticed her surprise. "It may not happen soon, but it will happen. You will practice here. He has been grooming you for this job. All that has happened in your life to this point has been because He is bringing you here to help us."

Kelly looked at Maria, then to William, and asked, "Are you sure about this?"

Maria looked at Kelly. "There is no doubt."

"But why now?"

William said, "We all allow our lives to be driven or even consumed by the concept of time. We make decisions based on how quickly something may occur or how quickly we may achieve something in our lives. But all of that is man-made, to satisfy whatever needs or wants we feel we must have. God does not recognize time as we do. He's not in a rush to accomplish anything, for He knows that to become proficient and productive with a talent or an ability, life requires a sufficient amount of time to learn basic skills. And when He feels we have acquired those skills and our attitudes also align themselves with the level of those skills, He steps in to take us to the next station in our life.

"We may spend our entire lives learning the skills necessary to do something, but in His eyes and under His plan for us, those skills may be used only once to accomplish something He wants done. Oftentimes, it is to benefit someone else. We don't pick those situations or circumstances. All we have to do to see an example of that is to look at the Cross and what it represents. He spent His life teaching and bringing biblical principles to life. And yet His life culminated in one act, one selfless act of sacrifice. But that one act created a foundation for all of human life. That act tied all human life together in some respect. All of what He does in our lives will do exactly that."

"Can it be as dramatic as the experiences in Rest Area 10?" Kelly asked.

"No," said William. "Oftentimes He simply whispers to us or nudges us in a certain direction, but when you learn how He teaches, your perceptions can become quite acute and accurate. He sees you as you are. After all, He is your Creator, and He knows quite well how you view yourself and the world around you. He will meet your needs and do so in a way you will understand."

He rested back in his chair and laughed a bit. "Even when we are slow to respond to His teachings, He stays with us. As I said before, He has been with you since you were here last as a small child. He has led you on your life journey to this point. You may not have been aware of it, but He has always been with you. Most of your decisions were made because of what He was whispering in your ear or how He touched your heart. And now He knows you're ready and able to practice in this type of an environment, under the differing circumstances that come out of Rest Area 10."

Maria looked to Kelly. "You know, Kelly, one of the most important things that William and I have both learned is that we necessarily don't have to try and find life or what we may think it should be. We have found, partly through Rest Area 10 experiences, that He brings life to us. And the interesting thing is that He often brings it to us in terms we can understand and in terms we can incorporate into our own life situation. He brings nothing to us that He has not prepared us to understand if we continually are in conversation with Him."

Kelly looked at William and then to Maria. "That's the key, isn't it? I mean our conversation with Him."

William said, "Yes, it is, but we must expect through our faith that He leads us in the direction that He wants us to go and not what we perceive. You see, He teaches us to move mountains on a whisper. Through Him, we can simply push our problems or the problems of others to the side and move on. But as I continually have said, He has prepared us through our prior learning and education on how the process begins. We have learned the basic treatments of health issues and problems, but now He teaches us how to heal and cure. Even then, it is still up to Him. The outcome will always rest in His hands."

Kelly looked at both William and Maria. "I have so much to think about now. I didn't expect this at all."

"He brought you here," said William. "He will guide you, and we will be part of that journey. Let's finish our supper, and then we can go back into the den and share more thoughts."

They began their meal again with their talk centering mostly on their house and how and why it was constructed the way it was. They had it built to reflect their thoughts on life and where they had come from and how it kept them balanced in life. They enjoyed the outdoors and nature. That's why they had chosen to build it off the road a half mile or so in a wooded area. It sat on a hill overlooking a valley below with a small lake.

The interior and exterior for that matter reflected the lifestyle they had chosen. The exterior was natural cedar, stained a dark red. It was small yet seemed very comfortable to Kelly.

Chapter 4

They all retired to the den, to a warm fire and more discussion. William sat on the hearth, opened the fireplace doors, and added a few more pieces of wood to the fire. He looked at Kelly as she sat down.

"A fire is an interesting piece of life. It has the possibilities to always keep us warm and, if we choose, to cook our meals. Yet if we abuse it, it can destroy us. We must understand it as it can create a place in our lives."

Kelly looked at him and at Maria. "You are very insightful, William."

"I have simply learned to listen to what He tells me. I have learned that He is never wrong."

Kelly looked at Maria, then to William. "I have a question."

"You may ask us anything," said Maria.

"I assume because of Him you saved a lot of people in the ER. I assume, also, you lost people in the ER. How do you internalize the loss of human life?"

Maria looked over at William, and he motioned for her to answer Kelly's question.

She began, "Our journey with Christ, because of Rest Area 10, dramatically changed the way we administered health solutions to our patients. When we first started practicing, the terms 'healed' and 'cured' we defined as meaning the same, but after our association with Rest Area 10, He taught us they are quite different in meaning. We could cure someone of their affliction, but we could not 'cure' them of the reason the affliction attacked them."

Kelly interrupted, "Did you learn how to cure them?"

"It took us some time to finally understand exactly what He was telling us," answered William. "We had to overcome our own internal problems so that we could really understand those we were working on. It was difficult at first because school had given us all the information we thought we needed to heal. Oh, we could stop the bleeding of an artery or set a broken arm or leg. But He demonstrated to us, through Rest Area 10, that we could not heal the person completely. Only He has the power to heal the Spirit, and without a healed Spirit, the body will remain broken. Neither Maria nor I can heal the Spirit, but through Him, we can. Through our faith in Christ, He comes alive in our decision-making. Our hands become His hands. Our thoughts are His thoughts. And how we heal someone is totally up to Him."

"Can you give me an example?"

"Yes," answered William. "That is the reason for Rest Area 10. You see, we didn't create that piece of land or the reason that people happen to stop there. He chose to create that for the people He deemed necessary who needed it.

"We will never fully understand the whys and wherefores of His thinking. We're not supposed to. We, just like the people that pull in there, are simply pieces to the whole story. And, like you, the story may take years to unfold. Like I told you earlier, time is not a factor in Christ's world. It has no meaning. We are the only ones that attach meaning to time. It is one of the greatest inhibitors of our abilities and talents, and we have to fight it daily not to allow it to consume us or yield to it and the effects it may bring to our lives and to our worlds. He will lead us. Always He will lead us, but it is always at a walk. Never at a run. Never.

"If we feel the need to run, it is because we have failed at listening to His instructions. But if because of our own misguided steps we should fall, He will extend His hands and pick us up. If we acknowledge our stumbling and ask for guidance and counsel, He will never fail in giving it to us. It may not come as we want, but it will come.

"You ask about an example. Every situation or experience that someone had that came out of Rest Area 10 is an example of how He can cure someone. We oftentimes create our own problems, but He uses them to heal us if we can understand what He is doing."

Kelly said, "How many experiences have happened in Rest Area 10?"

Maria answered, "There is no way to know because some did not directly involve us at the ER. Some we heard of secondhand, but even the ones we heard about were still miraculous happenings that Christ created for someone needing His help.

"William and I stopped to get fuel one time heading home, and there was a man in the convenience store telling the cashier of something that had happened to him in Rest Area 10. The man was shocked to hear from the cashier that there was no such place on Highway 61. At first, he wouldn't believe her, but after we substantiated her statement, the man stood there in shocked surprise."

"Did the man tell you what happened?"

"Yes," answered Maria.

Kelly asked, "Can you tell me about it?"

William smiled. "Yes." He then related the story.

*****

We asked the man if we could buy him a cup of coffee. There is a small cafe next to the convenience store. We were still in our scrubs, so we obviously appeared to be people in the medical field. We pulled our cars to the cafe and went inside. We sat at a table somewhat away from others, so we could talk openly about the man's experience. We introduced ourselves, and he told us his name was John and that he was kind of in shock about the whole experience. He asked us if we were doctors and worked in the area. We told him who we were and what we did. To calm him down a little, I explained briefly about Rest Area 10 and what had been going on there for several years. John seemed to be in shock or disbelief.

He sat back in his chair as the waitress brought our coffee. He looked at me and said, "I'm not sure how to explain this or even if I should, but I just have to tell someone and feel somewhat secure knowing that you are doctors."

I looked at him and said, "Whatever you decide to tell us, John, stays with us."

He took a drink of coffee and began.

"My life has not been what I had envisioned it would be. I have had many ups and downs. Many failures and few successes. I took over my parents' implement business and drove it into bankruptcy. I was married and had children, but after the loss of the business my wife left with the kids. I have no idea where they are or even what they are doing. I tried several times to correct my stumbling, but alcohol and drugs took me even farther down. I ended up basically living in my car or vacant buildings. I had nowhere to turn or anyone to turn to. So finally…" He paused and looked out the window next to us.

We sat in silence.

*****

Maria looked at Kelly. She carried on with the story.

*****

William broke the silence, offering comforting words. “John, we all have tough times, but there is always a way out. There’s always another road waiting for our footsteps. We just have to find it. Or if we are lucky like you, it may find us.”

John relaxed in his chair, took another drink of coffee, and started again. “I came to this part of our state because it is somewhat desolate. I thought I could just drive out here, find a lonely spot, and…” John stumbled emotionally, choked up, and began again. “I came here to shoot myself. I could no longer look in the mirror. I hated the face looking back at me. I made the decision to end my pitiful life. When I came around the curve in the road and saw Rest Area 10 with no people in it, it appeared to be the perfect place. I pulled in and up to the curb. There was an old-style outdoor toilet and some aged benches and picnic tables, but the ground surrounding everything seemed to be well cared for. In fact, the grass looked as though someone had recently mowed it. It gave me a weird feeling. I mean everything was old and appeared to be worn-out, but the grass and even the trees looked as though someone had spent a lot of time caring for them. I just shook those thoughts off, pulled my pistol from under the seat amid all the garbage, and loaded it.”

He looked at both William and me and shook his head. “Now that I think about it, it was stupid. I filled the magazine of the pistol. It would only take one shell. Anyway, just as I pulled the gun up, a pickup pulled into the rest area. It was a maintenance worker, I guess, for the rest area. He pulled in close to me, got out, and began unloading tools out of the back of his pickup. He said hi and started raking grass next to the sidewalk.

“I was so mad at having failed yet again at something. All I wanted to do was end my life, and I even failed at that. I put the gun under the seat again and was going to start my car and head elsewhere, but when I turned the key on, all the car did was click. I got madder and beat the steering wheel with my hands and said, ‘God, what’s next?’ Frustrated at the turn of events, I reached down, pulled the hood latch, and got out of the car to see what was wrong. When I lifted the hood, the battery was split in half. I started to slap the hood down, and the maintenance worker came up and ask if he could help. I looked at him and, in my desperation, said, ‘Nothing could help me now.’

“He looked at me with these amazing eyes that seemed to look right into me and said, ‘Oh, friend, nothing is ever as it seems. Sometimes, in our search for answers, we may find the solutions are very close to us. We just haven’t been looking in the right places and right direction.’ The worker motioned to the bench and said, ‘Why don’t you go over there and rest for a bit and allow me to look at your car. I sometimes have a knack for fixing things.’

“I looked at the bench and for some strange reason felt comfortable going over and sitting down while he worked on my car. He asked me if I had any pliers, and I told him there was a pair on the driver side floorboard. He opened the door up and finally found the pliers in all the mess that I had let accrue there.

“He looked at me and said, ‘You know, friend, sometimes the clutter we allow to accumulate in our lives can hide the answers to our problems. Sometimes it can benefit us to just try and straighten the clutter that we have allowed to accumulate. Oftentimes solutions may just appear from cleaning up the situations we find ourselves in.

In simpler terms, at times the clutter keeps our minds focused on the clutter and not on how to clean it up.'"

John looked at us both from across the table, rubbed his forehead with his hand, and continued, "It was the strangest thing. I lost my frustration and my madness. I sat on that bench and relaxed in the strange comfort of the worker's words. I had never felt quite like that. I felt as if someone really cared. I looked at the worker and felt unable to respond or even speak. I felt like I didn't have to. I didn't need to. I felt like I had to follow this stranger's advice.

"He told me to get back in my car and try to start it. I didn't question him or even say anything about the split battery. I simply got in the car, turned the key, and to my complete surprise, it started. I asked myself how that could be. I saw the battery. It was split in two. I saw it. The worker looked at me and said, 'It was just a loose cable.' He handed me the pliers and said, 'Go and have a better day. There may be something on the horizon for you.'

"As I left Rest Area 10, I was still trying to figure out what had just happened. I knew what I saw! The battery was split in two. Would I wake up from a dream? Maybe I had already shot myself? Was any of what just happened real? I looked in the rearview mirror, back at the rest area and the worker raking leaves, and thought, *Who is this man?* He then bent down to pick up a pile of leaves, and I was shocked to see my gun sticking out of his pocket, but you know, I didn't want to go back. I just knew I had to keep driving."

The man sat back in his chair and asked us, "Do you know what happened? I mean, you mentioned strange happenings in a rest area that apparently doesn't exist. Am I crazy? Did I shoot myself? Am I in another dimension?"

*****

Excitedly, Kelly asked William, "What did you tell him? How did you answer him?"

"I simply told him the truth. That whatever reason there was, God, the worker, wanted to save his life."

"How did he respond?"

Maria looked at Kelly and answered, "John began to cry and really couldn't speak, so William began explaining how God can work in our lives, that for whatever reason or reasons, God does at times directly intervene."

"How did the man respond?"

"He simply sat and cried for a time, but William continued explaining how Christ can move in our lives and that many times we may not know why or even understand His movements. John looked up from his tears in disbelief and said, 'I just don't understand any of this. Why would God take an interest in my life? I'm a complete failure. I am nothing. Everything I have ever attempted to do I have failed at.'"

Directing her question to William, Kelly asked, "How did you respond to him?"

"I told him that we all matter to God. He created us. He never wants to see His creation fail. He sees who we can be and not who we are at the present. I told him it doesn't matter what we are involved in or the depths of our stumbling. I told John that God can fix anything at any time. And how fortunate he was because in God's eyes, this was his time for healing."

"What did he say?"

William said, "He said he just didn't understand. That everything he thought about God or what he had been taught in the church he attended on an irregular basis about God didn't make any sense now. I told him that many churches don't really understand who God is either. He's not alone in those thoughts. I told him that Christ is more than just simply biblical words and verses. He is alive and doing quite well and, through our faith, is oftentimes very active in our lives. We may not always understand or even comprehend why or what He is doing, but He is here and He is always listening."

"What did John say?"

Maria answered. "He just sat there in disbelief for a while, drinking his coffee." She paused. "William told him that God just saved his life, and that because He did, God had a purpose for him. That all he had to do now was look toward tomorrow with hope and walk in faith, that as he does, God will provide the answers he needed.

"We both looked at John, and he just shook his head, still trying to understand everything that had happened to him. William told him that God had brought him here, that he did not come here on his own accord. He may have thought he drove his car to this part of our state and to Rest Area 10, but it was all God's doing. That God had a plan for the rest of his life and that for whatever reason that plan involves us as well."

Kelly looked at both William and Maria, paused as if she were trying to see something far away, and said, "I'm sure that John's story has more to it, but how many more were you two directly involved in?"

"There have been many, but the interesting thing is that even when we are not directly involved in the situation, somehow the story seems to always find its way back to us," answered William.

"Could you give me an example?"

William looked at Maria. "Tell Kelly the story of the young woman and the convenience store cashier."

"Okay. That's a good one."

Chapter 5

"We were working in the ER one afternoon, and a lady came in that works in the convenience store. She had slipped on a wet floor and fallen on her hand. The fall had bent her hand back, and she was concerned she may have broken it. William ordered an x-ray, and then we examined it. To get people to relax, William often strikes up a conversation with the person about their day or whatever he is led to talk about."

Kelly interrupted, "What do you mean, 'He is led to'?"

"We both believe that Christ is very active in our lives, even to the point of understanding when to ask a question or even in the direction that a specific question should go. We feel that He gives us the words to ask."

"Have you ever been wrong?"

William said, "When we began on this journey with Christ, as I have said before, we opened each day in the ER with a prayer that He would not only lead us in our medical techniques, but in our conversations as well. To answer your question, no, He does not make mistakes. He leads us, and we follow, whether it's with our abilities and talents as doctors or simply with our words."

Kelly sat back in her chair and shook her head. "I just have never heard of anything like this, ever. It is almost surreal. But I'm not saying I don't believe you because I most certainly believe every word you have told me."

William smiled at her. "Just allow yourself to absorb it. It is tough at first. I mean"—he looked over at Maria—"it was difficult for us at first. I mean experiencing your situation when your parents brought you here."

"Were you both, for a lack of a better term, religious before coming here?"

Maria smiled at Kelly and answered, "William's life is a bit unusual. He experienced something as a young teenager that laid the groundwork for what would happen much later in life. He has not told many about it."

"Why?"

Maria smiled at Kelly. "William will tell you."

"I chose not to say anything to anyone simply because no one would believe me, and maybe I didn't even believe it after it had occurred. I was between my fifteenth and sixteenth birthdays. I was out taking a hike in some woods I was unfamiliar with. Maybe I shouldn't have been there. Or maybe I should have taken someone with me. But anyway, I was there and had been hiking for about thirty minutes when I heard dogs barking. I really didn't think anything about it till it seemed as though they were getting closer. I had always heard about packs of wild dogs but never really thought anything about it. I mean I was a teenager. Nothing could harm me." William laughed. "Guess I was wrong. Anyway, I finally realized that they were probably trailing my scent and got scared, so I started running and then started running harder as it seemed they were getting closer."

Startled by the story William was telling, Kelly put her hand over her mouth and gasped. "My God, what did you do?"

William smiled. "That's exactly what I did. I called on God. I don't remember my exact words. I just remember asking Him for help." He chuckled. "I'm sure I was yelling at the top of my lungs. I kept running, but as I told you, I had never been there before. I had no idea what lay ahead of me. I just kept running. I kept pushing myself harder and harder. I felt as though I was going to pass out, but I kept hearing, '*Run, run, run* with everything you have.' So that's exactly what I did. I ran and ran, and the dogs seemed to be gaining ground on me. Just then I crested a hill and could see a fairly large creek below me, down the hill, so with all my energy I ran toward it, and I guess I planned on jumping it and leaving the growling dogs behind. I really had no idea what I would do when I got to the creek. But as I did, I screamed once more, '*Please help me!*' to, I guess, anyone that I felt was listening. At that point it didn't matter."

William looked away, as if viewing the past, closed his eyes, then opened them, and looked back to Kelly. She could see tears in his eyes.

He continued, "I ran directly at the creek, not really knowing what I would do. As I neared it, I heard that voice again. It was a man's voice, and he said, 'Don't stop. Trust me. Keep running!' So that's exactly what I did. I kept running. Right before I got to the edge of the creek, I closed my eyes and pushed harder. I didn't think about falling in. I thought about what the voice said, 'Don't stop. Trust me. Keep running!' That's exactly what I did. I kept running with closed eyes. My feet left the ground and landed on what I thought must be a bridge or something similar. When I felt the change, I opened my eyes, and to my surprise, I was on a bridge. I instinctively looked back over my shoulder and saw the growling dogs coming over the hill. I quickly crossed the bridge, but from panic and sheer exhaustion, I collapsed on the other side, but as I was losing consciousness, I heard something like rushing water. It was very loud, almost deafening. That was the last thing I remember till I woke up. I don't know how long I was out, but when I finally came to, I was lying exactly where I fell after I had crossed the bridge. Completely unharmed and just as I fell. No torn clothes, no bite marks. And no dogs anywhere. And there was one more thing."

"What!"

"As I looked back, there was no bridge, only the other side of the creek."

Kelly sat in silence. She started to talk but stopped.

Maria looked at Kelly. "I reacted the same way you have, Kelly. At first, when William told me, I did not know how to respond because I was like most people. I had never heard such a story, and I was very involved in church growing up, but it changed me. I began to see life in a different light. And with the stories coming out of Rest Area 10, it almost became commonplace."

Kelly dried her eyes and apologized for getting off track. "I'm sorry. You were starting to tell me a story about a young woman in the convenience store. Plus, I never let you finish the story about John. I just have so many questions now."

Chapter 6

Maria got up. "I think we need some tea. It may be a long night." She left the den for the kitchen.

Kelly looked at William. "How have you kept all this so secret? Did everyone involved just agree not to say anything? I mean with all that has gone on here, I would think word would travel."

William said, "None of us have made a conscious decision not to talk about it, but what we have done is to simply allow the Lord to work. This is His way of introducing people to Himself. Sometimes we are involved in the process, the experience. Sometimes we are not.

"And I would imagine that there have been others He pulled in to Rest Area 10 that we may never know about. It's difficult to say, but there is no doubt in my mind that if we are supposed to be part of the person's experience, He will bring us into view. None of us that have been directly, or even indirectly, involved in the experiences coming out of Rest Area 10 want to seek something that He does not want us to have. We are servants, Kelly. Disciples in a way. We allow our lives to be molded and bent by His will, by His direction and guidance. As I said before, that is why we start every day with a prayer."

"What do you pray for?"

"We all realize we work for Him. We, as I just said, are His servants. He works through us for the benefit of others, so we pray to understand what He gives us and how we should respond, both using our talents as medical people and as believers. We do not push Him on anyone that is not ready."

"How do you know someone is ready to listen?"

"We just have faith that He has prepared them before He brings them to us."

Kelly shook her head. "I think had I not been here as a small child, this whole situation might be extremely confusing. But, as you just said, I think He prepared me to hear what I have heard."

Maria came in with tea and cookies.

William looked at Kelly and smiled. "Maria is a great cook. Her cookies are to die for."

Maria handed Kelly a cup of steaming hot tea and a cookie. She sat next to William and placed their tea and cookies on the table between the chairs and looked at Kelly.

"Our greatest asset here, Kelly, is not simply our talents and abilities as medical practitioners. Our greatest talents reside within our faith. Without our unshakable trust in Him, we could never do what we do here."

"Tell me about the young woman in the convenience store."

Maria related the story.

*****

Well, Dorothy, the cashier that slipped and fell on her hand, just had a bad sprain, but she began telling William and me about this young girl that came in to the convenience store to get gas. The young girl had pulled up to the pumps and filled her car up like any normal person would. She came in to pay, and Dorothy asked her how her day was going. She told her that it was not going very well at all until meeting this very nice man in this rest area.

Dorothy looked at William and me and said, "You're busy here, and I don't want to take your time."

We looked at her and almost said at the same time, "We want to hear the story."

Dorothy looked at us and said, "You may not believe it. It's kind of far-fetched."

We both smiled at her and said, "Oh, we'll believe it."

So Dorothy started.

"The young woman's name was Kathie, and she told me that she was upset about the death of a friend and was just driving, basically with no place to go. She was just driving. She said she had neglected to notice the gas gauge, and just as she rounded this curve in the road, the car began to sputter. She looked at the gauge. It read empty. She looked up and noticed a rest area just ahead. As she did, the car sputtered more and began to die so she coasted into the rest area. It came to a stop just before it hit one of the concrete barriers in the parking lot. She said she was so upset, she just sat there and cried. Her whole day had just been so overwhelming she didn't know what else to do. Time had escaped her. She had no idea how long she sat in the rest area. But she looked up from resting her head on the steering wheel and noticed a maintenance truck had pulled in and a man seemed to be doing something there, like raking leaves. She got out of the car and walked over to him and related her story of running out of gas. She told me she got upset all over again at her predicament and began to cry. She said the man was very nice and told her that he carried gas in his truck and he could get her car going, not to worry, everything would be fine.

"Kathie said she looked at the man, and he had the most unbelievable eyes. She told me at the store she had never seen anything like this man before. I asked her what she meant. She said when she looked at him and into his eyes, he kind of just glowed. She said it was not a fear thing. She felt warm and safe when she looked at him. I asked her what the man looked like. She said he looked to be maybe in his sixties, with long, graying hair pulled into a ponytail. He was tall and appeared to be in good shape. I asked her if he said anything to her, other than getting her gas. She told me that as he got her the gas, he talked the whole time.'

"I asked Dorothy what the man said. She told us that Kathie said for some strange reason, because of the man's words, it seemed he knew what was going on in her life. She said maybe it was because he could tell she had been crying. Kathie told me it was like everything he said to her was just for her. She said it was the strangest feeling but not bad or scary. He made her feel at ease. In fact, after he put gas in her car, he asked if she was thirsty. He told her he had fresh-brewed tea in his truck and she was welcome to a glass. She said he didn't wait for her to answer. He just got the jug and poured her a glass. She said she had never tasted anything like it before, that she drank tea all the time. That it had an amazing flavor. She told me she asked the worker where he got it."

I looked at Dorothy and asked what was Kathie's response as to what the worker said. Dorothy told us that Kathie said the worker told her that it was just as important to use good water as it was to use the proper tea.

"Kathie asked the worker where he got his water. He answered her, saying he pumped it from a well right there in the rest area. He then pointed to an old-style pump just a few feet away. He told her he called it his living water. Kathie said she asked him why he called it that. She said he smiled at her and said all life requires water and the water there is the best this side of heaven. She told me she drank the entire glass, and he offered more. She said that as he took her glass to fill it up, he said, 'Let's sit on the bench here. It's easier to pour from my jug.' She said they both sat down, and as he poured, he began talking about how life is never as it seems. She told me that again it felt as if he were talking right to her and her life. She said it just seemed like he had all these answers, and they just made perfect sense to her.

"At one point she told me she looked at him and said it seemed for some strange reason he knew about her problems or at least her recent loss. She said he looked at her again with those penetrating eyes and told her that he had known people that had suffered loss before and knew what that pain was like and how difficult it was to deal with. In fact, he told her he had lost a son. But she looked at me and told me she had never mentioned anything about her loss.

"It was at that moment I asked her where this rest area was. When she told me, I looked at the other cashier as she looked at me. We both looked back at her and asked again where it was. She told us but also asked what was wrong. She noticed our strange looks back and forth to one another. I looked at her and told her there was no rest area there. In fact, I said, 'There is no rest area anywhere on Highway 61.'"

We asked Dorothy what Kathie did.

She said Kathie just stared at us for a bit in disbelief. "She looked away from us, as if trying to make sense of it all, looked back at us, and said, 'I didn't make it up. It was all very real. It happened.'"

We asked how she responded to her.

Dorothy said, "I started to say something, but she looked kind of surprised and said, 'I can prove it.'"

I asked Dorothy, "What happened?"

Dorothy said, "Kathie ran back out to her car, opened the door, grabbed something, and came back in the store. She held her hand up to show us the glass the worker gave her the tea in. I had never seen a piece of crystal that beautiful before in all my life. I looked over at the other cashier, and she was white. I mean she just stared at the glass. The light coming through it, I cannot explain. But I will never forget its brilliance. When the young woman held that glass up to show us, it looked as though it was a light itself. I mean it literally glowed. It gave both myself and the other cashier the chills. The hair stood up on our arms. We both commented on it to Kathie.

"Kathie looked at us and said, 'That's not all. Look at the bottom.' She turned the glass upside down, and I felt something pour over me like warm water. I could not believe what I saw. There, etched in the bottom of the glass, was a tiny Cross. I mean like a Cross associated with Christ. We were both speechless. 'But,' Kathie said, 'that's not all.' She turned the glass right side up and told us to look down in the bottom. We both looked, and to our surprise, we could not see the Cross. She turned the glass upside down again, and there clearly on the bottom was the Cross. The other cashier said she felt weak and sat down on the stool behind the checkout. We all looked at each other, but said nothing. Kathie looked at us and said, 'I don't know exactly what happened or is happening, but it does not scare me. In fact, I feel secure. I have never felt like this before in my life.'"

We asked Dorothy what happened next.

She looked at us, kind of with an apologetic expression on her face, and said, "I have to be honest with you both. I did not slip on the wet floor and fall. I asked Kathie if I could hold the glass. She handed it to me. And I swear to God, to both of you, when I took hold of that glass, I felt all the strength in my body fading. The next thing I knew Kathie and the other cashier were standing over me, asking if I was okay. I was dazed, but felt better than I had felt in years. The other cashier asked me what happened. I told them I did not know, but when I took hold of the glass, I saw a bright light and heard a voice say, 'Walk toward me.' I don't remember much, other than whatever happened to me or wherever I went was perfect, or at least that's the feeling I got from whoever was there."

Then William looked at Dorothy and asked, "What happened next?"

Dorothy told us they helped her up, and when she complained about her hand hurting, Kathie agreed to bring her here.

William looked at Dorothy with subdued excitement and asked, "Is she still here?"

Dorothy told us that she was.

William told her to please go get her. He wanted to talk to her.

Dorothy stepped out for just a bit and came back in with Kathie. She was cute with dark hair and a wonderful smile.

William looked at Dorothy and said, "So, Dorothy, this is Kathie?" He stuck his hand out to Kathie. "I'm William Scott. You have had an interesting day from what Dorothy has told us." He looked to me and back to Kathie and introduced them both. William then said to Kathie, "I didn't want you to leave without maybe explaining a few things to you. What occurred in Rest Area 10, to you, was very real. This kind of experience has happened several times to different kinds of people. It is an uncommon experience, but He has chosen to meet you on your terms for some reason. A reason maybe you and He only know of."

Kathie interrupted William. "Are you telling me that the maintenance worker was God?"

"That's exactly what I'm saying."

Kathie just stared at all of us for an instant and started to say something but stopped, then started again and stopped. Then she finally said, "I find all of this so difficult to grasp. I guess I wouldn't believe it at all had He not given the glass to me."

"May we see the glass?" I asked.

"Of course." Kathie set her purse on a chair, reached inside, and pulled out a beautiful crystal glass.

We all noticed that when she held it up for us to see, it had a glow about it. Maybe it was the way it captured the light and released it, but there was no mistake: it glowed.

"May I hold it?" asked William.

She handed it to him and said, "Turn it upside down and look at the bottom."

He took hold of it and was spiritually moved when the glass touched his hand.

They all noticed it, and Dorothy asked, "You felt something, didn't you?"

"Yes, I was expecting to." He turned the glass upside down and noticed the Cross on the bottom. He then turned it right side up, and looked in the glass. No visible Cross. He set the glass on the table near him, closed his eyes, and said nothing.

Kathie started to ask, but I put her finger to her mouth as if to tell Kathie not to speak yet.

In just a few seconds, William opened his eyes to the small group and said, "We all need to pray. Please, everyone, touch the glass and allow me to pray."

We all put a hand on the glass and closed our eyes.

William began. "Father, there are times in life that we don't understand. There are roads You take us down that we don't understand. There are experiences that we sometimes can't comprehend their meaning, but we thank You for them anyway, knowing that we will always learn from them. We thank You for everyone here and the experience that Kathie had in Rest Area 10, as we know it came from You. We pray that whatever meaning it has in her life, You would share it with her at an appropriate moment. We thank You for Your constant vigil over our lives. In Christ Jesus's name. Amen."

We all opened our eyes and were silent for a moment.

Breaking the silence, William said, "Rest Area 10 does exist for those of us that He decides need it. He does meet us there on our terms and for our moments of desperation or simply because He knows it is time." He looked at Kathie and Dorothy and continued, "You don't have to spend time trying to figure it all out because you never will. We can't comprehend God's motives or the reason why He appears to some and not to others. All we know is that He can, and He does." He looked at me, back to Dorothy, then to Kathie. "Many people have ways to define God that they can understand and somewhat internalize. Many use the Bible as God's Word. Which it is, of that there's no doubt. But that is just a part of who He is. He is limitless. He can do or be anything He wants to be at any time. And situations exactly like Rest Area 10 prove it."

He paused, waited, and spoke again. "When I closed my eyes just a moment ago, He told me something."

He looked at the group and paused. He closed his eyes again, opened them, and said, "Thank You."

He looked at the small group and continued, "God wanted us to know He is right here, right now with us at this moment." He picked up the glass, held it upside down to see the Cross, then asked us all to look at the bottom right side up.

Almost in unison, Kathie and Dorothy gasped, "My God!"

There in the empty glass, on the bottom, where it had not previously been, was a Cross. Both Kathie and Dorothy teared up.

William calmed them. "I know this may seem overwhelming, but He always gives us something to hang on to, something to remind us of just how special we are to Him. We are so valuable in His eyes. At any time in our lives when we feel we need something to sustain us, to give us strength, we can find it in Him. All we have to do is ask. He always answers us, always." He looked at Kathie and continued, "I know you're just passing through our town, but I would encourage you to stay the night. Maria and I will take you out for supper. We would like to share and discuss this with you some more if you would like?"

"I would love that."

Chapter 7

Kelly looked at Maria, then to William. "Did either of you not believe an experience or story coming out of Rest Area 10?"

William looked at Kelly with warm eyes and responded, "We believe that Christ brings people to Rest Area 10 for a reason. We may or may not know what that reason is. It's really not up to us to figure that out. Why someone is in the situation that leads them to Rest Area 10 is beyond us. We may find out about it later as we have in certain situations, but it would be difficult to understand all the whys and wherefores. We are simply led to offer help that's within our range of understanding and the scope of our talent and abilities. If He leads us further, then He will provide us with a level of insight that is required to understand. All of this, all that happens, and all that occurs is because of Him."

Kelly interrupted, "But what if all that is going on in that person's life is directly related to their own inabilities to correct their own mistakes?"

"What you have to understand," said William, "is that each of us can make any number of mistakes that seem irreversible and without a solution. But that's simply a human frailty, a fault that lies within us all. At times, the mistakes we have made seem unsolvable, but through His eyes and through His understanding, the solutions are simply waiting for us to discover them."

"What do you mean 'discover them'?"

Maria responded, "He requires us to put forth an effort. To work, if you will, to try and find a solution. Look at it this way. Christ came to earth not as God but as a man. He came to understand all that anyone of us must face and endure, but He also understood that life requires work. That life takes effort to unfold. He knew that to be successful, there must be the physical component. There must be sacrifice to promote a level of understanding. He understood work, what it would accomplish, and to a great degree the avenues that that work would illuminate to each of us and direct us toward."

William added, "What you must understand is that Christ often speaks to us through experiences and situations that grow out of our work." He paused, relaxed in his chair, and continued, "Simply put, understanding Him in our lives comes from doing. It may seem at times that we are moving in the wrong direction, but there again, those feelings may be His help to change our course, to improve our movements."

Kelly exhaled as if she was frustrated. "I believe what you are both saying, but at times it seems somewhat confusing to me." She looked at both William and Maria. "But there is no doubt that He has brought me back here to learn from the both of you." She smiled at them and offered a quiet thank you. She looked at them and asked, "How much faith does it take to start making steps in a positive direction toward what Christ wants to accomplish in our lives?"

William got up, walked to the fireplace, and picked up something off the mantel. He walked back to Kelly and handed her a small glass jar with a black lid on it. It was no bigger than a small medicine bottle, the kind prescriptions come in.

"Can you see the seed in the bottom?"

"Yes, but it's very small, almost not noticeable at all."

William sat back down. “Everything in this room is one hundred times larger than that small seed. It would be insignificant in most people’s eyes. It has no real meaning in the scheme of life, but in relation to the size of faith, faith that small and insignificant can move mountains. Christ promises us that. Size matters not to Him, but our belief in what we can accomplish through Him does. Because our faith in Him only requires one small insignificant step toward what He desires in our life. We may think that step is insignificant, but He does not, and that is all that really matters.”

Kelly sat back in her chair and relaxed, as if she were deep in thought. She looked at them both, began to ask something, but paused. “With all that we have talked about and all that you have shared, what is the most important characteristic that any of us could possess?”

“That’s easy,” answered William.

“What do you mean?”

“Christ calls us to be like Him. We are to mirror Him. Sadly, though, the most important character trait any of us can ever possess is the same character trait that many of us fail to possess, but if we are lucky enough to gather our strength through our faith and make it a part of our lives, it will clean our house of all things that clutter and corrupt our lives. It will push everything that weighs on us to the bottom of the Cross. And there, in that spot where His blood covers the ground, His blood also covers our failures, our weaknesses, and our shortfalls. That trait, Kelly, is forgiveness. Without it, we are only half of what we could be—if even that.”

Kelly looked at both William and Maria. She looked around the room. “How many things in here represent your journey with Christ or are something connected to Rest Area 10?”

William answered, "Everything in here, Kelly, depicts an aspect of our journey with Christ through Rest Area 10."

Kelly looked at William questioningly. "Could you explain that?"

"Yes. This room and everything in it represent something that happened directly from someone else's experience with the rest area. The room itself was built by one man whose life was not only saved in Rest Area 10 but was also given a new direction because of what happened there."

"May I ask who?"

William smiled. "It was John, who we spoke of before. He wanted to end his life in Rest Area 10, but Christ saved John's life in Rest Area 10 and from there gave him a new direction for him to go."

Kelly looked at the both of them and, with excitement in her voice, said, "I want to know everything. I want to understand why Christ would do all these things for the people that were fortunate enough to stop there."

Maria looked at William, then back to Kelly, and smiled. "That's why you are here, Kelly. You did not come here of your own accord. Just like all the people that have stopped in Rest Area 10, you were all brought here for purposes far greater than yourselves. There are no dead-end roads in Christ's world. There are always alternative paths to follow that will take us to where He wants us to go. Sometimes, He will allow us to stop in a place to rest or to collect our thoughts, but He will always guide us to another place."

William got out of his chair, walked to the fireplace, opened the doors, stirred the coals a bit, and added a couple of pieces of wood. He looked at Kelly. "Our lives, Kelly, are just like this fire. Because of Christ and His love for us, there is always a spark waiting to be ignited. It may not be noticeable with the naked eye, but it is there, and it does exist."

Kelly interrupted, "You're talking about Christ?"

"Yes. Christ is always just out of eyesight. He promised us that, and He will always fulfill those promises to us. Always!"

She looked at them both. "I'm just a little confused. There are those that talk about God and all that surrounds Him. I'm not sure I understand it all." She looked away from them toward the fire, as if to gather her thoughts, and continued, "You both talk about Christ. You rarely mention God. Why?"

William looked at Maria as if to say go ahead.

Maria thought for a second, then began, "Kelly, Christ told everyone that no one gets to the Father but through Him. It's just that simple. We must first build a relationship with Christ before we can understand God and all that resides with Him. We must have that relationship before we can grasp what He has in store for us. It's not really that difficult. The most difficult aspect is our ability to let go of most, if not all, of what man teaches us about God because most of what man teaches benefits only man. Christ told people not to lean on their own understanding but to accept His guidance and counsel. And He is never wrong—ever!"

William rose from his chair. "We can resume our discussion tomorrow over breakfast. It's getting late." He looked at Kelly. "You can stay with us tonight." He pointed to the sofa near the fireplace. "That's a roll-out bed and is pretty comfortable. You may sleep in here. There is a bathroom just around the corner. Feel free to add more wood to the fire, and if you're thirsty, you may get anything from the kitchen."

"Are you sure it's okay?"

"We wouldn't want it any other way," said Maria. "Just make yourself at home here. If you need something you don't have, please just ask us."

Kelly looked at them both. "I don't know what I expected to happen when I came here, but I am so glad I did. I don't have the words to explain how I am feeling right now."

"We totally understand, Kelly," said Maria. "Take your time. We are in no rush here. Christ will help you absorb it all, and I'm sure He will give you guidance and counsel."

William looked at her. "Would you like to pray before we all retire?"

"I would like that very much."

William motioned to them. "Let's kneel by the fireplace."

The three of them walked up to the hearth and knelt in front of it. He placed his right hand on the stone and Maria placed her hand on top of his and Kelly placed hers on Maria's.

"Let's bow our heads to our thoughts and His love," said William. "Lord, we are so thankful for Your presence in each of our lives and thank You for the strength to share our thoughts with one another. Thank You for bringing Kelly here, and we just ask that You open our hearts and minds to Your wishes and wants for her in our lives. We ask these prayers in Your Name as our Lord and Savior."

William raised his head and eyes to Maria and Kelly. "Right now, at this moment, the warmth of His Spirit and heart invades every part of each of us." He looked at the couch. "Let's undo this and set it up for you. Surprisingly, it does sleep fairly well. The mattress is quite firm."

They all worked together in taking the cushions off the sofa and unfolding the bed.

Maria looked at Kelly and said, “If there’s anything you need, just ask.” She smiled at Kelly and continued, “We are both so glad you came. Sleep well, and we will continue our discussion over breakfast.”

William added, “Please treat our house as your own. If there’s anything you need from the kitchen, feel free to get it.” He smiled at her. “I would also encourage you to look around this room. Look at it all and read anything you wish to. We will see you in the morning.”

They left the den and headed to their bedroom.

Chapter 8

Kelly sat on the edge of the bed and looked around the room. Everything in this room was directly or indirectly created from an experience or situation emanating out of Rest Area 10. There were all kinds of things—paintings and small statues, books in bookcases, and magazines on the tables.

Her attention was drawn to bookcases with glass doors attached to both sides of the fireplace. One book stood out in the case on the left side. It was a lighter shade of green, almost the color of leaves. It was as if it were calling to her. It almost appeared to have a light on it, illuminating it and separating it from all the other books.

She rose from the bed and walked to the case, opened the glass doors, and pulled the book out. She held it up to look at it. It had a simple title embossed on the cover, *Living my Life*. It was by Dr. William Scott.

For some reason, tears filled her eyes. She felt as if something were taking hold of her, something that was kind, compassionate, and loving. There were no audible words, but she distinctly heard, "This is a vessel of life, a container to drink from."

She looked around as if to see someone, but no one was there. Only the crackling from the fire filled the silence of the room. She sat on the bed, closed her eyes, and prayed softly.

"Thank You, Lord, for saving my life so many years ago, never forgetting who I was and for giving me all that my life has required to get me to this point."

She sat on the bed in silence for a few minutes more. Feeling as if someone were watching her, she slowly opened her eyes to the room. She felt as if she were expecting something or someone. The room had an atmosphere of warmth. It seemed to wrap around her. It washed across her, and from a dark corner, an image of a man in a beautiful white robe appeared. She was not scared or shocked. It was a feeling of unimaginable peace and security. She simply absorbed His thoughts. His language went straight into her and settled in her spirit. For a moment, she rested in what she heard and saw. Then the image was gone, but not the feeling of His presence.

She sat in stunned silence, accepting the fact that Christ had directed her whole life and He had simply reaffirmed His promise to her this night.

She looked down at the book she held and sat thinking about the last several hours. She opened it to the first page. It was blank except for these few words right in the middle. They seemed to stand alone, to possess their own strength and power, to convey something greater.

She read them aloud to herself:

> You may have the tools with which to confront your chosen profession and possibly life, but achieving success with these tools requires the correct application and administration of their usage.
>
> Remember, anyone can have a hammer, but not everyone knows how to drive a nail. The

> power you possess to swing that hammer and to drive that nail is not yours alone. Your Faith controls the direction of your hammer, and your Faith controls the power of your swing.

She sat and read those words over several times. She read them once more and thought, *What an opening for a book about one's life.* She raised her head and looked once more around the room. She thought, *Most houses are decorated with different things of the occupants' life. Or they may not have anything on the walls at all. Those houses may simply be a dwelling place, a place to lay one's head and at times eat. But this house, and especially this room, was something totally different. This house and this room contained living examples of the expression of one's life. The things hanging on the walls, sitting on the shelves, and hidden in the bookcases are living results of one person finding or actually being found by the greatest power that exists in this world. In fact, this room is the work of faith in this man's life, but it's not one person's single step. In fact, this room contains the examples of years of planning, building, and moving people in the proper direction to achieve the desired results. I am surrounded by the connection that must exist between a person, their life, and all that was placed before them. Simply, this room and the contents are the connection between Christ and His creations.*

Again, she looked around the room and sat in wonder of what it all meant. Then a thought struck her. It was as if someone touched her shoulder and gave her a gentle nudge.

She looked around the room and thought, *Everything is connected here. But not simply because it is here. It is connected. It is held together by a force far greater than anything on this earth. It is what holds all things together, even when all things seem to be falling apart. Man cannot break it, cannot tear it in two, cannot destroy it. It is but a thread, a tiny insignificant aspect as some may think, but our world cannot exist without. It is what our world was built around, and no man will destroy it. But it may consume man at any moment.*

Her thoughts went deeper than the room. They went deeper than the world beyond this house and beyond the land that lay at the doorstep to many people's lives.

She looked up to the fireplace once more and noticed a beautiful wooden Cross. She spoke out loud to the room and to the One she believed was there.

"You know, Lord. I guess Your disciples felt the same way when You were dying on the Cross. They felt abandoned. They felt their world was collapsing. All of what You had taught them they felt was useless. They felt the power being drained from their lives that Your presence gave them."

She shook her head, looked down at the book, turned the page, and as before found only one paragraph in the center. She read it once, then twice.

> For some, this day may bring the end to a journey. For others, this day may be the start to a new one. For some, there is no other fork in their road, no other course of action. Sometimes, in the time it takes one tear to fall to the ground, all life ceases, and yet all life will begin again. And, as we realize, our happiness that began with a flurry ends with a touch of sadness. But the trees that lost their leaves in the Winter will leaf again in the Spring. Life will transform itself, and once again our sadness will be but a distant memory.

She looked up from the book and around the room. Speaking to the silence that filled it, she whispered, “Thank You.” She lay down on the bed, placed the book on her chest, and closed her eyes to her thoughts.

Chapter 9

William and Maria changed their clothes and crawled into bed. They pulled the large handmade quilt up and on them. They sat against the headboard and looked at each other.

William spoke first. "You were right, Maria. She would come back, and she did." He reached under the quilt grabbed one of her hands, pulled it on top of the quilt, and continued, "Isn't Christ amazing? It is so awesome how He has interwoven all these lives to accomplish what has transpired in all their lives." He looked at her. "Look how he brought us together. Who could have ever thought that we would accidently meet in a rest area that didn't exist and ultimately build a life together, helping people who benefited from an experience occurring in Rest Area 10?"

William scooted closer to Maria, bent down, kissed her. "I could never have done what we have done. When we met in Rest Area 10, sat on that bench, talked, and shared our thoughts with that worker, something was ignited within each of us that prior to that point we were unaware of. Maybe it was simply lying dormant in each of us. Maybe for many years we were like packages that He was filling with everything we would need when He finally did bring us together. And then, in those first moments as we explored each other and grew closer, those two packages were slowly unloaded and placed into one single package containing things that would make that package work. We kept those things we needed and, at His urging, discarded what was unnecessary. Some things we needed in our single life, but now they were no longer of value to us."

He held her hand tightly, rested his head against the backboard, and sighed a little. "We have talked about that meeting for years and will continue to do so for many more. Neither of us knew, prior to pulling into a place that doesn't really exist, what was about to happen or even why it was to happen. But He did. Christ brought us there at the appropriate time. From opposite ends of this country, He had constructed each of our lives with everything we would need to literally begin a life in medicine together. Not only had he given each of us the talent, ability, and experience to start this journey, He also instilled in us what is possible and what can occur."

Maria looked up at him and smiled. "When I pulled into that rest area, I had really no thought what was about to happen. I mean I simply wanted to stretch me legs and walk around. I had been driving for so many hours. It seemed a perfect spot. You know, dear, we didn't pull in there on our own accord. He pulled us in there. I will never stop being amazed at what He does and how He does it. We made the choice to pull in there, but the most phenomenal thing was that He created the entire scenario to bring us together, for us to meet. He was building a life for us, and we had no knowledge of it, at least at that moment in time." She shook her head, squeezed his hand, looked in his eyes. "Think about it, William. He brought it all together. He brought our lives together. Not just as people, but as doctors with hearts to understand and spirits to accept His guidance and counsel."

William looked as though he were searching their history together, looking deep into the past. "I was sitting there on that old wooden bench talking to what I thought was a maintenance worker about my life, about how I loved being a young doctor. Then when you pulled in and got out of your car, he brought you into our conversation. And from that point on, our lives slowly began to evolve." William looked at Maria and laughed. "I think we were totally oblivious to what lay right before us. But He knew. He controlled the conversation to introduce each of us to the other and that we were both going to the same hospital to work in the same ER. And now so many years later, look what we have accomplished through Him. Look how many lives He has changed just because He first changed us."

She looked back to him and squeezed his hand tightly. "I had no idea back then where I was really going, what it was going to be like when I got there, or even those I would be working with. But He did. Christ knew exactly what was going to happen and when it would happen and what would be the outcome. I could never have envisioned how this would all turn out. Remember what He told us?"

William looked at her and smiled. "Neither of us will ever forget that. His words made much more sense to both of us after we had time to think about them."

"You know, dear," began Maria. "I don't think at that moment in Rest Area 10, we fully realized what was happening at all. But after they came in with that child and all that happened, our lives moved in other directions. The worker looked at us and, with eyes that went straight into us, said, 'Everything behind you is the past, but the past is your source of information, your experience in understanding your future. But the source of your energy and all things needed to begin each day lies within what you both see at this moment. The problems you will face you will never face alone, and you will never not come up with an answer. It may not be the answer that you're looking for, or it may not be the solution you were expecting. But it will be what is needed at the time it is needed.'"

William went over in his mind what happened that day in Rest Area 10.

*****

He was getting sleepy after driving all day. Although he was excited about starting a new job as an ER doctor, his thoughts and expectations began to trail off into drowsiness. He came to a curve in the road, and just ahead was a rest area. He woke up a bit and decided what a great place to stop and rest or maybe even sleep. As he pulled in, he noticed that it appeared to be an old-style rest area. There was nothing fancy here, that was for sure. It had a wide parking lot with benches and picnic tables with roofs over them in the grassy areas. There were no soda machines or fancy buildings. It was just a rest area. A place to take your mind off the road or simply to unclutter your thoughts. What a great place.

He pulled up to a concrete parking barrier and shut the truck off. He leaned back against the seat and closed his eyes to the world outside. How long he had been asleep, he did not know, but when he woke up, there was a maintenance worker raking leaves in the grassy area in front of his truck. He got out, stretched, and said a hello to the worker.

The worker returned a greeting and walked up to William and stuck his hand out. "They call me Peter." He smiled at William and continued, "When I drove in, I noticed you sleeping and tried to be as quiet as I could. You were out of it."

William looked at him and shook his hand. "I'm William. Glad to meet you, Peter. Thanks for being quiet. I have been driving all day and got a little sleepy. Your rest area came along at just the right time. I really fell asleep." William chuckled a bit.

Peter asked, "Are you thirsty?"

"I sure am."

Peter pointed to an old-style hand pump to their right. "The water that comes out of there is the best-tasting water this side of heaven."

"Sounds good to me."

"I've got a cup in the truck. I'll pump you some out."

"I'll help."

Peter walked to his truck, grabbed the cup, and met William at the pump.

William worked the handle up and down as Peter held the cup. Once it was full, Peter handed it to William. He took a drink.

"This does have a great fresh taste to it. It kind of reminds me of one of the wells on my grandfather's farm. It always had such a fresh taste to it as well."

"Are you just passing through, or are you staying a while?"

William stretched again and took another drink. "I hope to be staying a while. I'm the new ER doctor at Blessing Hospital in Arcadia."

"Well, you're almost there. You obviously have been there and interviewed?"

William laughed a little. "That's the funny thing, Peter. They hired me based on my resume and a phone interview. This is my first visit to this area." William scratched the side of his head with his free hand. "The whole process of me getting hired in Arcadia seemed almost weirdly predestined."

"What do you mean?"

William looked at Peter. "Can we sit on that bench?"

"Oh, sure."

They walked to the bench and sat down.

William stretched a little and began. "When I first applied for this position, everything I did just went off as clockwork. It all just sort of fell into place. I told one of my mentors about how smoothly it was going, and he commented that it was obviously the place I was supposed to be."

"You're probably right."

"Have you been around here all of your life, Peter?" Before Peter could answer, William continued, "It seems like a nice place, from what I understand. I mean the interviews were all very warm and friendly. Everyone I spoke with was very cordial and considerate. It was almost like talking to old friends. Like I had known these people forever."

Peter smiled. "It is a very nice place. It sometimes seems as though I have been here forever. This place creates a good feeling, and strong bonds can be established here."

William looked around the rest area, yawned, and stretched again. He looked at Peter. "This place looks and feels like it's been here a while. Almost like it may have been built back in the fifties. I would assume it has been?"

Peter looked across the grass and up to the sky. "Oh, it's been here for a very long time. Many people have come through this place on their way to somewhere else. It's a place to just relax, to rest, and, for some, I would imagine, to plan for tomorrow."

"I would imagine there's more truth to that statement than one realizes."

Just then another vehicle pulled into the rest area from the east heading to the west just like William. It was a small SUV, and as it pulled up, they could see a young woman in it.

She got out; bent down to stretch; raised back up; and, with a cheery smile, said, "Good morning, gentlemen. This is a beautiful spot." She walked up to them, and as she looked around, she said, "This place looks like a picture out of the past." She smiled at Peter and William.

It was obvious to her who Peter was. His dress was that of a maintenance worker. *But who is this nicely dressed man?* she thought. He appeared to be of a similar age, maybe early forties. His hair was longer than most but pushed back. He had what looked like a Carhartt shirt on with jeans. *Kind of a country-type guy.*

She started to introduce herself, but before she could, William interrupted, "When you mentioned picture, a recent memory brought another picture into to view. You're Maria Cavanaugh, aren't you?"

She was surprised at his comment and answered, "Why, yes, I am. How did you know that?"

William stuck his hand out. "I'm Dr. William Scott. We will be working together in Arcadia at the hospital." He shook her hand and smiled. "I was given a picture of you by the board that hired me. I'm sorry if I startled you."

She returned his smile and the firm handshake. "I am so glad to meet you. I've read a lot about you."

"You're too kind."

Peter interrupted their thoughts. "Kind of a wonderfully relaxing place to meet your fellow worker, isn't it?" He looked at them both while they still were enjoying the moment. "Sometimes a meeting like this can lead one to believe that there could be more going on than one realizes."

William turned to look at Peter. A strange movement flowed through him as he momentarily thought of what Peter had just said. He paused while looking at Peter.

Maria noticed it. "Are you okay?"

"I'm fine. Just a little tired from all the driving."

But as he said that, he remembered a time many, many years ago when that same movement ran through his body. A time when all things stood still. A time when something seemed to clear his mind and take hold of him. A time of trust. A time when his confidence must be placed in something far greater than he realized. A time when he realized his life was not his own. His life belonged to the Creator of all life.

He looked at Peter, then to Maria, returned to the moment, and said, "Well, this is a pretty cool chance meeting," and smiled.

"Yes, it is. I'm glad this rest area is here," answered Maria.

*****

As they lay in bed, his thoughts returned to the moment. William looked at Maria. "Tomorrow will be an interesting day, no doubt."

"It will be a day well spent, in a way only He could give us."

William agreed, leaned down, and kissed her.

They snuggled into each other and closed their eyes to the night but not to their most intimate thoughts.

Chapter 10

The fire popped and crackled, and Kelly stirred to the noise that woke her. As she sat up, she forgot about the book on her chest, and it fell to the floor.

She had fallen asleep without turning off the small green lamp on the nightstand beside her. It illuminated the book on the floor. When she looked down and started to grab it, she noticed it lay open to another quote. She reached for it and brought the words into view. Kelly read it once, then again, and finally once more. She shook her head as if to clear her mind of sleep, got up, and sat on the floor with her back against the bed.

Dad was right, she thought. *William is much more than just a doctor.* She looked around the silent, dimly lit room, and whispered to the emptiness. "There is much more here than I realized."

She raised the book a tad bit higher to see the words more clearly and read them again.

> What we find, we find not by accident, but by the diversions that bring us to the point that we can understand why we are here, what is before us, and the importance of what we must do.

She looked at the book and laid it on her lap. *I came to the right place*, she thought. At first, when her dad told her about Rest Area 10, she had hesitated but it was his dying wish that at least she would come and see. That's why she did, and he was right. *There is much more to this place, much more.* She closed the book and allowed her mind to wander. *What other situations and experiences have grown from this place? How many other people's lives have been affected directly or indirectly by a tiny piece of earth and grass? It is a place of simplistic grandeur, where thoughts float in on a breeze or arrive from thunder that shocks the prairie that surrounds it.*

A knock came on the door. It opened, and Maria stuck her head in and asked, "Ready for breakfast?"

"Yes. That sounds perfect. Can I help?"

William was standing next to Maria and said, "You sure can. What would you like?"

"Whatever you have planned is fine with me."

He said, "We usually have hot tea with fruit and yogurt and maybe fresh bread. How does that sound?"

"That's fine. What can I do?"

Maria spoke up as they walked into the kitchen. "The pot is on the stove. You can fill it with water and heat it up. The tea is in the cabinet to the right. There's a variety in there. Anything you choose is fine with us."

Kelly answered with a simple yes and began her task while William and Maria prepared everything else.

While filling the teapot, Kelly looked at them both. "I have a question."

"Ask whatever you want," said William.

Kelly looked at him while turning the burner on and setting the filled teapot down. "What was the first situation that started the whole process of Rest Area 10?"

William looked at Maria. "Why don't you answer that one, dear?"

She smiled at him, looked at Kelly, and started, "That's the interesting part of our story. I mean William's and my story. As fate would have it or as Christ prepared it, our story too began in Rest Area 10. We both stopped there, William first and I followed a few minutes later. We did not know each other prior to that. We both knew we would be working with another doctor. After our initial meeting there, we believed, after much discussion, that it was a place of informational moments for us. Christ was introducing us to our futures without, to a degree, us knowing it. He was introducing us to each other."

"Did you know what was happening at first?"

"I had no idea who William was when I first got out of my car to stretch. But as we started talking to each other and the worker, telling him who we were and where we were going, William recognized my name and face from my picture, I mean from my interview photos. I didn't know who William was because I did not have the same information. Well, after we had found a motel for the night and temporarily got settled in, we decided to go out for supper that night. We both felt it a good way just to get to know each other in a relaxing situation outside of the ER. We asked the motel owner about a place to eat. The man asked what we were looking for, and we said something organic if it was available. He suggested a small trendy little cafe that offered an organic menu. We went there and were not disappointed. It was very good. Our conversation started just by filling each other in on our pasts. Where we had grown up, gone to college and med school. It was kind of neat."

"In what way?"

William was filling three bowls with fruit and looked Kelly's way. "We found out that our parents had both attended the same private college, a small college nestled along the Mississippi River in the town of Canton, Missouri. It's called Culver-Stockton College. It's a neat place, with an interesting history. It sits atop the river bluff. Anyway, our night began with an evening of great stories. Some our parents had previously shared with us. Some we heard for the first time from one another. We laughed at our parents' stories, and at one point Maria looked at me and asked, 'William, do you feel as though there is more here than meets the eye? I mean, it all seems like there is some kind of plan here.'"

Maria was slicing bread and looked at Kelly. "At that moment, Kelly, something just struck me. It was almost as if I was having several conversations at once, or at least hearing or listening to others' thoughts. William and I talked about that. That was kind of the start for us. I mean, little by little that night over supper, we began sharing our philosophies on living, on life and death. It became clear that we were more alike than different. We were both brought up in Christian households, and a strong work ethic was instilled in us both. It also seemed that we both had a commonsense approach to medicine, the administration of it."

William interrupted, "We almost talked till the cafe closed. Our conversations just seemed to flow from one topic to another. At one point, I felt like I needed to say something to Maria about my faith."

Maria placed the bread on the table as William set the bowls of fruit down. She looked up from the table to Kelly, who was getting the tea from the cupboard. "I had never heard someone explain their faith stories like William did. I was kind of captivated by them. Not because they were unique or something I hadn't heard before, but because they were much like my own. I looked over at him and just stared at him for a second." She laughed and looked in his direction, and with a big smile on her face, she said, "I really think my silence made him uncomfortable, but that wasn't it, and I knew it."

Kelly looked at William. "Did you say something? I mean because of her silence?"

"I think Maria and I were both thinking the same thing at the same time. Our silence was not because the situation was uncomfortable. It was quite the opposite. Our conversation had become very relaxed and easy. I think we both realized at the same time that it seemed we had met before. It seemed that our lives, to a degree, had mirrored each other. Somewhere deep inside both of us, we realized in that silent moment that Christ had brought us together for a reason."

"What did you say?"

William looked at Maria, and both appeared lost in their memories.

Maria spoke first. "Oh, Kelly, I think he was just smitten with my looks." She laughed, and they all laughed.

William chuckled again. "Honestly, I probably was." He paused. "Let's eat."

They all sat down at the table, and Maria asked if Kelly would like to give a blessing.

"Sure." Kelly asked a simple blessing, thanking Christ for the food, the morning, and the discussions they would all share in.

William said, "Amen."

As they began to eat, Kelly looked up from her meal as if she had forgotten something. She looked at both William and Maria. "I have something in my car that I want to read to you. My father gave it to me not long before he died."

"What did your parents do?" asked Maria.

"They had always run a small cafe. It was something they both enjoyed. Dad and Mom said it was a piece of life that seemed to fill their own needs. They were simple people, not wanting much from life. They enjoyed others. They enjoyed the stories of people that came and went through their doors. They always enjoyed sharing their faith with anyone, whether they were regulars or were just passing through their town. Their cafe was small, not more than six or seven tables, but there was always a lively discussion at one of them that Dad or Mom was usually drawn to. Sometimes, people would meet there on their comings and goings through life, and something would happen."

William interrupted. "Sorry for interrupting, but how did your parents meet? What brought them together?"

Kelly looked at them both. "After I read Dad's note he gave me, you'll understand. Let me go to my car and get it." Kelly got up and hurried out to her car and returned with an envelope.

As she opened it up and took out what appeared to be very worn pages, she said, "I have read this over so many times, and every time I do, I tear up. This is an experience Dad had in the cafe when he was there as a young traveler, long before they were the owners. There is no doubt in my mind that this is why Mom and Dad bought it. They felt it was what they had to do in life. It was kind of neat. Mom worked there while putting herself through college. It was where they first met, and what happened that day to Dad brought them together. I know you two will love this." She began, "These are Dad's own words from many years ago." She started to read and stopped, paused, and started again.

*****

Many would never believe what I am writing, but I wanted to write this story down, mainly so I would not forget it later in life.

I was heading back to college late one afternoon and decided to stop at a small cafe for supper. It wasn't very big, but I had stopped there before, for breakfast or just to have coffee while returning to college. The parking lot was always full because the townspeople or passersby knew of the good food. It was run by a couple that always had a smile and a kind word for anyone.

As I got out of my car, I realized I might have to wait for a place to sit down. When I got inside, my first thought was correct. It was full.

But a young waitress about my age came up and apologized that they were full but a table would open up soon.

At a table nearby, an older gentleman sitting alone said, "You can sit with me if you want."

I looked at the man and said, "Sure."

The young waitress turned to me and said, "I'll get you some water and a menu and be right back."

I sat down, thanked the man for letting me join him, and stuck my hand out to shake his. I said, "I'm Robert," and the man said, "I'm Paul. Glad to meet you, Robert."

I thought as I looked at him, he had the strangest eyes. They were warm. He looked like he could be anyone's father or grandfather for that matter. I had the strangest feeling when I looked at him. It wasn't bad. In fact, looking at him made me feel good. I kind of shook my thoughts off as he said, "You look like a college student on his way back to school."

I smiled politely and said, "You're exactly right. I am returning to school from a visit home."

"What year are you, and what's your field of study?"

"I'm a junior and studying culture theory."

Paul smiled and spoke. "Oh, you like studying about the rise and fall of civilizations?"

I was a bit surprised at his knowledge and said, "By your comment, you have an understanding of my major then."

Paul took a drink from his cup. "I have some expertise in your field of study. It wasn't what I majored in in college, but it has always interested me somewhat. My focus was more in philosophy and religion. I became involved in what could pull people together or, on the negative side, what could drive people apart."

"What did you come up with?" I asked.

He looked at me with those eyes again. I can't explain how I reacted to them, just that I did. It was like I would believe anything he told me. It was just the strangest feeling. Maybe it was just our apparent age difference that made me so receptive to what he said or how he said it or simply my respect for someone older. He reminded me of a professor, a wise man. Someone who had already been to where I was heading.

Just about the time he started to speak, our waitress came back with my water and a menu.

She looked down at me and said, "I'm Nicky. Can I get you something else to drink, and do you already have an idea of what you want?"

She had the prettiest blue eyes.

I answered, "Yes, I'll take coffee and a hamburger with crispy fries."

"I'll get them right out for you."

As she walked away, Paul looked up and over his cup, smiled, and said, "She's a nice young lady, probably about your age. She told me earlier she was waiting tables to put herself through college." He took another drink from his cup and said, "Okay, back to your question. It has always been my belief that we can be led astray from what life should be to what life should not be. There is more power in the world that lies just beyond the horizon than the power most of us immerse ourselves in."

I interrupted him, apologized, and asked, "Then why do we? Why are we carried away?"

He took another drink from his coffee and replied, "You probably don't want to get in this deep of a conversation. I sometimes get carried away talking to those that will listen."

I thought, *There is something to this man. He is a man of substance, of meaning.* I replied, "No, please continue. I'm enjoying your thoughts."

He continued, "In our culture today, we place so much emphasis on what we want to surround ourselves with to somehow satisfy our desires. We become oblivious to actually looking for those things that may enable us to understand what is before us."

I interrupted him. "You're talking about materialism in a way."

"Partly, yes. But there is more. We are given the ability to see and understand things, but sadly those desires I just mentioned cloud our sight and shade our understanding in colors of gray. We somehow lose the vibrant colors that can come from life."

I looked at him and smiled. "That's a cool way of stating it."

Nicky had arrived with more coffee just as Paul was talking. Not wanting to interrupt his thoughts or his words, she stood and listened. As he finished, she said, 'I'm sorry for listening to your conversation, but that's a great explanation." Breaking the intensity of the moment, she offered us a coffee fill-up. She looked at Paul and apologized for interrupting and said, "You seem to have some answers to life."

He looked at her and smiled. "Oh, I've just been around a while." He chuckled and continued, 'So many want to make life more complicated than it actually is. Many begin to put too much trust and attach too much value to situations and circumstances that really have little to offer. They may satisfy basic needs, as some may see their needs to be, but really, most, if they were honest with themselves, still come away hungry for more."

Nicky looked at Paul and asked, "What would satisfy their needs?"

"Well, first they would have to realize what their needs really are. Sadly, as I said earlier, most do not."

I looked at both Paul and Nicky and asked, "Then how are people supposed to find out?"

Paul smiled in a compassionate way and said, "In most circumstances they find it by going through a bad experience or situation. They find it out of conflict or from desperation. They find it because they haven't found it through anything they had previously tried. That last act of desperation unleashes all that binds them up emotionally and spiritually, and finally they *may be* ready to learn, but I do stress *may be*."

Nicky had a strange look on her face. She looked at Paul, paused a bit, and said, "I have a question, but first I need to pour coffee and check on my customers."

Paul smiled. "Okay."

She left our table to wait on her other customers and fill coffee cups up.

I looked over at him and said, "You're very insightful. What exactly is it that you do, if you don't mind me asking?"

Paul smiled at me. "My life's work has simply been helping others find their way."

I looked at him and asked, "How many ways exist?"

"Only one." He stood up. "Well, Robert, I'm a little late for my next appointment, but it's been fun meeting you and chatting."

I was kind of surprised he was leaving. It seemed too abrupt. I was anxious at his leaving. I had more questions. I looked at him and said, "Do you have time for one more question?"

But before I could ask, he answered, "Always look and listen. But above all, love." He stuck his hand out after putting his coat on and said, "It was good to meet you. I enjoyed our conversation." He looked over to where Nicky was waiting on customers. "Nice girl. She has a lot to offer the right guy. You take care, Robert. Maybe we will meet again someday." He left the cafe and me to my thoughts.

But as he did, I started to sit down at the table and realized he had left his gloves. I grabbed them and went to go catch him, but something fell out from between them as I picked them up from the table. Nicky was close by and turned when she heard the sound of something dropping. She looked toward the noise and noticed something on the floor by my table. Bending down, she grabbed it and brought it up for me to see. I looked at it. It was a tiny little Cross.

"That's strange," said Nicky. "Where did this come from?"

"It fell out of Paul's gloves as I picked them up from the table to return them to him." I looked at Nicky and said, "Let me catch him, and I'll be right back. He just left."

But when I walked out of the cafe, he was gone. I thought, *He just left. He can't be gone.* I looked all around, but he was not there. I just stood there for a second, trying to understand what had happened.

Just then Nicky stuck her head out the cafe door and asked, "Did you give them to him? Where did he go? I had a question for him."

I looked at her, and I know I had a kind of lost look on my face and said, "He's gone. I don't know how he could have gotten away so fast. He just left."

I shook my head as Nicky said, "That's weird. Why would he just abruptly leave?"

"I don't know."

We both walked back inside the cafe. I sat back down at my table and fingered the small Cross.

Nicky sat where Paul was sitting, looked at me, and said, "A chill just ran down my back." She looked at me with this blank stare and asked, "Can you tell me what just happened?"

I looked at her. "No, I can't. I have no idea. I mean this nice older gentleman invites me to sit with him and eat. It's the only open chair in the whole cafe. We have one of the most interesting conversations I have ever had, in very few words, and then he literally disappears."

In a strange but satisfying way, Nicky said, "I'm getting off soon. If you're still here, can we talk a little bit about this? Or do you need to go?"

I smiled at her. "Oh no, I'm not in a hurry. I would like very much to talk with you about this."

She stood up to go finish her shift, and as she did, I noticed a $5 dollar bill on the table under Paul's coffee cup. I pointed to it and said to Nicky, "Paul left you a tip."

She reached down, lifted the cup up to get the five dollars, but as she did, she noticed a small piece of white paper with something written on it.

I asked her, "What does that say?"

Her face turned white as a sheet. She stared at the paper and looked at me with a blank stare, tried to speak but couldn't.

I asked her, "Are you all right?"

She simply pushed the paper to where I could see what was written on it.

I looked down at it and could not believe what I was reading. I rested my right arm on the table and put my hand to my mouth to steady myself and my thoughts. I looked up at her, into her stare, and read the words aloud, "The answer to your question, Nicky, is there is only one way. And that way is through Jesus Christ."

Nicky placed her hand over her mouth, then took it away, and said, "How did he know what I was going to ask?" She turned, still with that blank stare on her face and a little exasperated. She said, "Let me finish, and I'll be back. Now I *have* to talk to you." She shook her head as she walked away.

I thought as I watched her, *I don't understand what just happened either.*

*****

Kelly looked at both William and Maria and said, "That's what brought Mom and Dad together. Isn't that a great story?"

William answered first. "Yes, it is. Christ is amazing. We must always remember where our focus must be, what it needs to be centered on. Then, and only then, will our lives unfold as they should."

When he said, "Unfold," the word caused Kelly to recall a passage from William's book; and she quoted it.

> Life is like a blanket. And Christ is the weaver. It doesn't matter if the threads are tightly woven for warmth in the winter or loosely woven to breathe in the summer. The weave cannot be

> broken or torn in two. Sometimes, the blanket must be shaken rigorously to dislodge something that doesn't belong between the threads. But no matter how the blanket is used or if it's stored for certain times in a year, it always retains its strength and purpose.

"We never wanted anything to move our focus away from what He wanted us to do. It was never a slippery slope for us." William looked over to Maria and back to Kelly and continued, "Maybe had Maria and I not met at Rest Area 10 early in our careers, things might have played out differently, but when we arrived here, for the most part, we had already passed through most of the pitfalls that can come from a life in medicine. And then, slowly through the effects of being connected to Rest Area 10 and all that came from those experiences, we evolved into the doctors and the people we are today."

Maria looked at Kelly and said, "It was a process of 'becoming' for us. Each day, whether it was a normal day in the ER or something special or exciting, we were mentally and emotionally evolving into who He wanted us to become. It was almost as if we had no choice in where we were going. We were simply being led. And because of our faith, we followed. Each situation allowed us to use what we had learned previously to coming here." She looked to William, then back to Kelly, and continued, "We had learned all the basics of ER medicine and were well versed in all the tools necessary for positive outcomes in our patients. But Christ allowed us to learn, through our faith, how to apply all of that. He taught us how to pull everything together to make our brand of medicine work. Sometimes, the outcomes were not positive, at least as some would say. But through Him, some level of understanding was always reached."

William looked at Kelly. “You know, Kelly, it’s not always about the process of living, of staying alive. At times, in some very emotional moments, He taught us that it can be about how to die well. I know that may seem incongruous to what we do, but dying well can be the end goal to living well. Many don’t want to approach it that way, but it can change one’s whole life perspective if one can get to that point.”

Kelly shook her head. “I realize now why I came here.”

William looked at her. “And why did you?”

“I had no choice. I had to come here.”

Just then William’s phone rang, interrupting their discussion.

He answered, “This is William.” Listening to the voice on the other end, he answered, “We’ll be right there.” He turned to both Maria and Kelly. “That was the ER. A couple just came in, and the woman was complaining about falling on concrete and possibly breaking her arm.” He looked at Kelly and, with a level of subdued excitement, said, “You’ll accompany us. This may be interesting.”

They all left the breakfast table and hurried to get to the ER.

As they were all walking out of the house, Kelly was reminded of what she had seen in William’s den the previous night.

She looked at both William and Maria and said as they got into William’s car, “Something happened in the den last night that I need to share with you both.”

William turned as he backed out of the driveway and looked at Kelly in the back seat. “Please tell us. We’re all ears.”

Maria turned to face Kelly and smiled.

“Well, I was sitting on the edge of the bed. I had turned the light down and was resting in the discussion that we had had. I bowed my head and thanked Him for saving my life in Rest Area 10 so many years ago and for all that He has done to get me to this point. It was quite emotional to finally realize that, yes, Christ was in control of my life and, yes, He had brought me to this place again and to you both. I sat in a quiet peace that seemed to wrap around me and invade every part of my being. I could feel Him, and when I looked up, out of the darkness of one corner of the room, He appeared. And what He said and what I heard was simply that I would never be alone, that I have never been alone. And then He was gone, but the strong feeling, that invading presence that wrapped around me at that moment is right here, right now."

Maria looked deeply into Kelly's thoughts and answered, "And you will never be without His presence nor without His wisdom. It does not matter what you're involved in or the problems that you are facing. He is here. Always, He is here." She paused, then spoke again. "Just remember, Kelly, it is your faith that connects you to His voice and to His direction for you in your life. Most don't really know how simple life with Christ can be. It is an everyday, every-minute experience into listening for His guidance and counsel. It is simply relying on Him and waiting. And at the exact moment when you need something from Him, He delivers."

William's phone interrupted their conversation.

"This is William." He listened. "Please just have her arm x-rayed. We will be there in ten minutes. Thank you."

They arrived at the hospital, parked, got out of the car, and walked to the ER entrance.

William spoke to both Maria and Kelly as they walked in. "Just a short prayer for guidance and understanding with these people." He looked at Maria and continued, "I have a gut response about this couple. They may not be the happiest. Not sure what Christ is telling me, just that they may have other issues we may have to deal with."

All three walked into the ER. A nurse met them and ushered them to the waiting room where the couple waited. The nurse handed William the x-rays, but before they opened the door to the room, the nurse said, "Dr. Scott, there is one thing I think you need to know. They told us that she slipped and fell on the concrete sidewalk in a rest area."

They all looked back and forth to each other.

"Thank you," said William. He reached over, grabbed Maria's hands, and whispered softly, "Patience and guidance, Lord."

Chapter 11

William opened the door and allowed Maria and Kelly to enter before him. As they did, they found the couple sitting in chairs beside the examining table.

He stuck his hand out. "I'm William Scott. This is my wife Maria. We are both ER doctors here." He looked to Kelly. "This is a friend of ours, Dr. Kelly Brown. She's also an ER physician."

The man stood up and stuck his hand out to shake William's. "I'm Devon Maxwell, and this is my wife Meredith."

They all shook hands, and William said, "I wish we could have met under better circumstances." He looked at the couple and asked as he placed the x-ray up on the lighted panel, "Can you give me a brief explanation of what happened?"

Devon began to speak, but his wife interrupted him.

"Well, this never would have happened if we had not made this ridiculous trek out here to this godforsaken piece of land he wants to buy!"

William glanced at Maria, then back to the couple.

Maria knew exactly what William was thinking. They had often seen this kind of reaction between couples where an accident was involved. One or the other always blamed the other for the situation. She smiled at William, knowing that he could handle what lay ahead.

He directed his question to Devon. "How did your wife fall?"

But before he could speak, she interrupted again. "It's all his fault. I slipped only because he has been so infuriating over this whole buying a farm thing." Condescendingly, she continued, "He wants to leave a million-dollar job and become someone who plays in the dirt for a living. How dumb is that? He wants to become a stupid farmer!"

William looked down at her. "I grew up on a farm, Meredith. I myself think it's a great idea."

She grunted aloud, "Huh," and turned her head from them.

William looked at the x-ray as did both Maria and Kelly. They all looked at each other. Each questioned what they were looking at. William began again by questioning Devon.

"Devon, can you tell me exactly what happened to Meredith?"

Devon looked at his wife, who was still looking away from the group, and said, "Well, we were driving here and regrettably were having an argument over the land and us possibly moving out here. I needed to take a restroom break, and as we came into a curve in the road, I noticed a rest area up ahead."

William's and Maria's eyes met at the same time. Kelly looked at both of them with raised eyebrows. Each knew what the others were thinking.

Devon noticed their expressions. "Is there something wrong?"

William apologized, "No, please continue."

Devon began again. "Well, I told Meredith that I was going to stop and use the restroom, but when we pulled in, I quickly realized that this was not an ordinary rest area. There were no modern facilities. No buildings to speak of. There were only a few picnic tables and an old-style outdoor toilet. We were still arguing as I pulled in and stopped the car. There was I guess what would be called a maintenance worker there raking leaves also. He looked our way as we drove in and parked. Meredith was mad that the rest area was not modern and commented that I couldn't even pick the right kind of place to stop."

Devon looked at Meredith and told her he was sorry for losing his temper and getting mad at her. She turned for an instant, looked his way, scoffed, and looked away again.

He continued, "I regret saying what I did, but I was mad, and my temper got the best of me, and I told her to go to hell. She jumped out of the car and screamed back, 'You first!' In her apparent anger she slipped on the concrete barrier in front of our car and landed on her arm. The maintenance worker was close by, and right before she fell, he said, 'Neither of you wants to go there. It's not a nice place at all.' He noticed her fall, quickly came to her aid, and offered assistance in helping her up. It was apparent to both her and me that her arm might be broken. At first, Meredith did not want the man to touch her. In fact, she said some pretty hateful things to him, but the worker just responded that maybe he could help. She turned away from him. But I told her to let the man look. The worker just looked at her and said, 'You know, Meredith, sometimes help can come from the unlikeliest of sources and can be closer than we think. I will not hurt you.' He smiled at her and continued, 'You've already done that to yourself. Anger is rarely an answer to anything.' She would not look at him but did allow him to examine her arm. And as he did, he began talking. His voice was soothing."

Devon looked at his wife, who was still looking away, and continued, "As he talked, he very gently stroked her arm. I could tell as he did, her pain level seemed to subside. The muscles in her face were not so tight. In fact, I asked her if she was feeling better. She said the pain seemed better. I looked at him, and he had this amazing expression on his face. I can't describe it to you. I just know I had never seen such a look on anyone's face before. The worker looked at Meredith and told her in a calming voice that his father was a farmer of sorts and that working the land always put him in a beautiful place. The worker said, 'It's almost spiritual, Meredith. I mean what the land can do to a person once they immerse themselves in it and allow it to unfold around them. You begin to feel part of something and not apart from something. Your outlook may change, and it may surprise you how you may change.'"

Everyone was surprised when Meredith began to cry.

Devon looked at her and was shocked. He started to say something, but Meredith interrupted him and sobbed, "How did he know my name? And how did he know what we were arguing about? We never said a word to him, nor did we tell him our names."

Devon looked at her, then to William, Maria, and Kelly, and said, "That's correct. How did he know that?"

William looked at Maria and Kelly, then back to Devon and his wife. "I think you need to sit down, Devon. I need to explain something to you that you both may find very difficult to believe."

First, he looked at Meredith's x-ray on the lighted panel. "You can clearly see where a break occurred." He pointed to it. "But that is a healed break. It's not a current one." He looked at Meredith, still in tears, and asked, "Have you ever broken that arm before?"

"No, never."

"I didn't think so."

Devon looked puzzled. "What is going on here?"

William looked at them both and began, "You both may find this extremely difficult to accept or believe, but the rest area you stopped at does not exist as most would understand."

Devon interrupted, "What do you mean 'doesn't exist'? Hell, we were there. We know it exists."

Meredith's demeanor had completely changed. Sobbing, she asked, "Can you explain to us what you just said?"

William looked at both Maria and Kelly. "Over the course of many years, we have had people come to us here at the ER for various medical reasons who had stopped at what is commonly referred to as Rest Area 10. And all of the people said it was a rest area just after the curve on Highway 61. But, in reality, it is not there. There is a curve, but there never has been a rest area. "But for those that were lucky enough to be pulled in there, it does exist."

Meredith interrupted, "What do you mean 'were lucky enough to be pulled in there'?"

William said, "You may find this difficult to believe, but you were brought to that spot for a purpose. I don't know what that purpose is, and maybe at this moment, you don't either. But there is One Who does."

"And who is that?" asked Meredith.

William looked at both Devon and Meredith. "The worker that was there."

Devon snickered. "What's he got—special powers or something?"

Maria looked at William, then calmly said, "He has much more than special powers. No one is above Him. No one knows more than Him. And"—Maria paused—"and you were lucky enough to have met Him. Most never do. Most only speak to Him through prayer."

Meredith began to cry again. "Oh, my God! How is this possible?"

William answered, "Only through Him is it possible. Maria and I have learned that we don't make the rules. We simply follow His lead. No matter which direction He pushes or pulls us, it's always the right direction." He continued, "We know this is difficult to believe, but there have been many situations quite similar to yours that have occurred in Rest Area 10. Your story is not the first and prayerfully will not be the last." He looked at Maria and reached for her hand. "Our story began in Rest Area 10, as did Kelly's."

Devon had a blank look on his face but moved closer to Meredith. She wiped her eyes and reached for his hand as he grabbed hers.

Meredith looked at William, Maria, and Kelly and asked, "Could you explain this to me? Could you explain why God would intervene so directly in our lives?"

"I cannot," answered William. "But we can help you both to understand how He can work in our lives to get us where He wants us to be. And I know that He does not see us as we appear to be because of certain situations. He doesn't see our anger or even recognize our hate. He sees us as we could be through Him. We are all simply works in progress. Some of us make it. Some of us don't. He comes to us where we are, not where we could be, because He knows we can't get to where we could be without Him. Without Him we stand in darkness, and at times, we allow anger and hate to consume not only our thoughts, but also our speech and our actions."

William paused, thought for a second, and continued, "And the amazing thing is, Meredith, no matter what we say or even do, He never gives up on who we can become through Him. Plus, He does not have a memory of sorts. I know at this moment you may feel as though, because of your previous anger, you don't deserve what He has done for both you and Devon. None of us can ever earn His presence in our life. It is a gift He gives us, and that gift came at a heavy price."

Meredith looked up at William first, then to Maria and Kelly. "I know this may be a strange request, but do you have time to talk to us about this?"

"You know, Meredith," began William, "if this would have happened during the week we couldn't, but He knew our weekend would be open for discussion."

Maria followed. "We would be happy to meet with you both over lunch and share our stories with you. We think it may help you to understand the journey you both are about to embark on. I mean that is if you decide to stay in our area."

Meredith looked at Devon through teary eyes and squeezed his hand. "I guess maybe this is where we are supposed to be." She squeezed his hand again and looked into his eyes. "I'm sorry. I haven't been very nice to you this whole trip."

William looked at both of them. "Tell you what. Let's make sure you're okay, Meredith. Then how about we all go out for an early lunch? It will give us a chance to get to know each other a little better. Maria and I can give you a little history into Rest Area 10."

Meredith looked once again to Devon. "We would both appreciate that very much."

William looked at Kelly. "Would you like to examine Meredith while Maria, Devon, and I do some paperwork?"

"Sure."

As William, Maria, and Devon left the room, Kelly looked at Meredith and asked her to sit on the examining table. As she did, Meredith said, "This is all real, right? I'm not dreaming this and at some point I'll wake up?"

Kelly held Meredith's arm up and slowly moved her hands around it. "You're not dreaming. This is very real. What has happened to you today is such a gift. God sometimes allows things to happen just to get our attention on the things that really matter in our lives. He does it to change our course in life. Some of us accept His leading, others don't."

Meredith looked at Kelly. "You too had an experience in Rest Area 10?"

"I did, but I was just a child. My parents kept it secret for many years, expecting that no one would believe them. Dad was dying and wanted me to know about our experience there. He also wanted me to know a few other things that had happened in their long life together. I am very fortunate that they wrote these experiences down, but surprisingly they kept them secret, for the most part, until after they both had died."

"Why do you think that is?"

"Both Mom and Dad were always focused on allowing me to find my own way. That's not to say they weren't right there always ready to help because they were, but they had always taught me to listen to that voice just beyond eyesight, that voice that exists just beyond the horizon of our thoughts."

"You mean God?"

"Yes."

Kelly held Meredith's arm up a bit. "Do you have any pain at all?"

"No, none."

Kelly smiled at her. "You appear fine. Whatever you did when you fell in anger, He healed you in love."

Meredith teared up again.

Kelly reached for a Kleenex and handed it to her. "It's all right. Christ can bring us to tears, but those are good tears. They cleanse us and can wash away our frustrations." She smiled. "Let's join the others."

Chapter 12

Kelly and Meredith walked out of the examining room and met the others in the waiting area.

William looked at Meredith and Devon. "You're going to be fine, Meredith. I realize this all may be a lot to understand at this moment, but if you would like, we can all go out for lunch, and we can give you some insight into your experience and why it may have happened. There's a very nice restaurant not too far away that offers a diverse menu."

Devon said, "We would greatly appreciate that if you can take the time for us."

Maria looked at them both. "Time is what have when an explanation is required. You can follow us."

They walked to their cars and drove to the restaurant. It was a simple building reclaimed from a previous business that had failed.

As they were getting out of their vehicles, Meredith looked over at Devon and touched his hand. "I am sorry for who I have been. I know it may be difficult to believe right now, but that's not my personality. I lost track of the person you married." She cried softly. "I know that person that I lost contact with is the person you fell in love with and married."

He smiled back at her, grabbed her hand, and squeezed it. "It's not all your fault. The angry and hateful moments that occurred between us were both our faults. I have often failed to explain my reasons to you for what I have done or have wanted to do. I'm sorry." He smiled at her. "You're right. That person I fell in love with and married is still here."

She reached over and kissed him. "We can do better. We can try harder."

They got out of their car and followed William, Maria, and Kelly into the restaurant.

It was not very big inside, but it was decorated in a natural motif with pictures of flowing streams and beautiful mountain vistas. Devon and Meredith felt relaxed.

She looked around and felt strangely at home in the situation that surrounded her. She thought, *Where have I been? Have I been lost and confused with all that I wanted to surround myself with? Did I choose to attach value to a world that offered little of real value? Who am I? Who was I?*

A strange but familiar voice from somewhere inside herself, but yet outside herself, softly whispered, "You were simply momentarily lost, but now you're home. I will provide what's necessary to keep you here."

She looked around, expecting to see someone, but no one was there. Or was there? A picture a little out of focus formed in her mind, a picture of the maintenance worker in Rest Area 10. His voice was silent, but His smile and message were not. She stopped walking and put a hand to her mouth as a tear escaped her eye.

Devon stopped walking also and put a hand on her shoulder. "Are you all right?"

She looked over at him, moved to his side, and kissed his cheek. "I'm more than all right. I fully realize that it may not seem to be an honest thought, given our past, but thank you for bringing me here."

A waitress broke their emotions of the moment. "You all may sit anywhere you like."

They moved to a table that would seat them all and sat down.

William had noticed the prior movements between Devon and Meredith and said, "Once He brings us back in contact with Himself and each other, amazing things can and do happen. He rebuilds and realigns our focus away from what was distracting us to how we can be attracted to what is necessary in our lives. We must yield to that if we want to experience what He has prepared for us." He smiled at them. "Explained simply, He brought you both to a point where the only thing that is required past this point is your dependency on your faith, your dependency on Him to meet all of your needs. And He will."

Meredith looked at Maria, then to William and Kelly. "We are very lucky, aren't we?"

Maria answered, "You are very fortunate to have found Rest Area 10. You may regret the hostile conversation you and Devon had, but it did allow for your experience in Rest Area 10 to transpire. Your anger and reaction to Devon's wants and his hurtful response to you created a road that led you both to Rest Area 10."

William interrupted, "There is one thing that we all realize at some point in our lives, our spiritual lives more pointedly."

"What's that?" asked Devon.

"Many of us, at some point, come to the understanding that He can move us to where we need to be, even though we may have given up or thought our situation was impossible."

Meredith looked at Kelly. "You're much younger than William and Maria. Do you understand all of this?"

Kelly sat back in her chair and exhaled. "You know, Meredith, none of us needs to exhaust ourselves moving in the direction of our

Lord. He comes to where we are. He knows us better than we know ourselves. He knows how we need to be fed, and He knows at what point we are hungry. The vehicle that gets us to where we need to go is simply our focus on Him. How were arrive there and in what condition can be totally up to Him."

Devon looked at William. "Does it ever…" He paused, thought, and began again, "Does it ever get confusing?"

"Sure, but the more we try, the more we listen, ultimately the better we become at listening and understanding what He is telling us."

Just then the waitress came back, looked at William, and asked, "Will all of you be eating, Dr. Scott?"

"Yes, we will." He looked at everyone. "This is Pam." He then introduced Pam to Kelly, Meredith, and Devon.

She handed them all menus and took drink orders. "I'll get your drinks and return for your orders."

They smiled as she turned to leave.

Devon looked across the table to William. "You told Meredith and me you would explain Rest Area 10 to us. I take it to mean that there may have been many experiences coming out of this place?"

"There have been many. There are those that we know about, but we all assume that there could be just as many that we don't know about. Some who have pulled in there we may never know about. Some may only need an encouraging word. And they may never understand what happened to them. Rest Area 10 may, in reality, be a complete mystery to them."

Maria said, "We don't fully understand His motives, partly because we are not required to or we don't have the mental or emotional capacity to. We may not need to be part of His process in their lives. William and I realized that He chose us, at times, to be involved. Other times not."

Meredith looked at Kelly and asked, "How do you see all of what happened to you? How do you internalize it? How do you make sense of it? I'm sorry I have all these questions. I'm just trying to get to a point where I know what's going on."

Kelly smiled at Meredith. "You know, Meredith, I don't think any of us here, whether it be myself, William, or Maria, can actually say we fully understand. Because we can't. We can't see what's ahead of us. We can't see what He has planned for us, but we can have faith that whatever it is it is perfect for who we are, where we need to go, and how to get there. It can be a mystery to us. But not to Him. He has given us so many promises through His word, the Bible. It can be a starting point for both you and Devon."

Maria looked at both Meredith and Devon. "I can promise you both that if you start reading Christ's gospels, He will open your eyes and ears to His thoughts for direction in your lives. These are promises He makes to us, and gladly for us all, He never goes back on a promise. And the very interesting thing is He makes His words come alive through what we are doing. Sometimes at the exact moment we are doing it. There's one thing more." She looked at both Devon and Meredith. "He never makes a mistake. Ever."

Just then Pam came back and began taking their orders.

Devon asked William, "What's good here?"

William smiled and chuckled. "Everything is. Most of it is organic or grown in the area. We have eaten here for many years and have never been disappointed. We enjoy the spinach salad with nuts and fruit, but we also enjoy the grass-fed beef dishes. Hardly any of it is fried, but if it is, it is done in peanut oil. Like I said, you won't be disappointed."

They all ordered to their personal preferences. Some settled for salad and a sandwich while a couple ordered soup and a sandwich.

As Pam left their table, William looked at Devon and Meredith. "There is a real need in our community for fresh produce and fresh vegetables. We do have a great farmers' market, but we need a more diverse selection to satisfy the needs of everyone that calls our town home. If you are looking to raise and grow food to some degree, I would encourage you to explore this option. Financially speaking, your greatest investment would simply be your land and a limited cost of basic infrastructure. It wouldn't be like investing as larger-type farming enterprises are required to. Plus, you would be slowly immersing yourselves in our community and the subculture that exists here.

"Because of the farmers' market, you would have the pleasure of meeting many people who live and work here. You would become part of us, part of our community, and those benefits may help you understand the new direction your life may need to go. And there would be an added plus in this type of a close community. You would be able to receive help if and when you needed it. Also, the new road you are now both on, His road, will bring more and more things into focus. He will provide the experiences you need and the people who can help, and He will provide them all at the exact moment you need them."

Meredith unexpectedly reached over and placed a hand on Devon's arm. "That may be exactly what you're looking for and maybe exactly what we need right now." She smiled at them all and, with a quizzical expression said, "Maybe it's what He has for us?"

Maria smiled back at Meredith. "You may be learning how to take your initial steps right now through our discussion. Oftentimes, this is how He leads us."

"What do you mean?" asked Meredith. "I'm sorry, but this is all new to me, and I need more explanations."

Maria said, "Oftentimes, Christ teaches us through the experience of someone else, of someone who has already made positive steps in the direction Christ wants them to go. This type of teaching helps us to develop the level of confidence that we need personally, to persevere, to keep moving forward."

"I understand that explanation. Thank you. That makes sense to me."

William spoke again. "It's really not that difficult, Meredith. As we let go of who we were and move toward who He wants us to be, through faith, it becomes easier."

Just then Pam began bringing their food and placing it before them.

Maria looked up at Pam. "This looks great, Pam. Thanks to whoever is cooking."

"I'll pass that on."

Just as they all began eating, a lady approached the table from a nearby one. She looked at them and said, "I apologize for the interruption, and I apologize for listening to your conversation. But when I heard something about Rest Area 10, I couldn't close my mind nor my thoughts to you. Again, I apologize for interrupting your meal and conversation, but a few years ago I had an experience in that same rest area. It was quite moving and ultimately changed the direction of my life."

William stood up, introduced everyone around the table, and said, "Please join us."

"Oh, I don't want to intrude. I just wanted to pass on my comment."

Kelly stood up and grabbed a nearby chair. "Please sit. Our conversation is all about Rest Area 10. Anything you have to add, we would love to hear it."

The lady sat down and introduced herself. "I'm Lucy Erring, and I just came back to town to visit Rest Area 10 and had hoped to stop there and possibly meet the maintenance worker who I talked with a few years ago. But when I drove out there, it was no longer there. I just figured they had torn it down. It was kind of an old, antique-looking place anyway. I came here to the restaurant to relax and somehow relive my experience there, to put it all in perspective. Then I heard someone at this table mention Rest Area 10. Again, I'm sorry, but I just had to listen to what was being said." She looked at William, paused, and swallowed hard. "Does this place really exist? I mean Rest Area 10?"

He answered, "Yes, Lucy, it does exist. It is there for the unsuspecting traveler who needs what can be found there. It is anything to anyone that needs something at a specific time, to change something in their life. It's not something that they necessarily have to ask for. In fact, they may not even realize they need the answer they are given." He looked at her. "We would all love to hear your story. We really would."

Chapter 13

As they all began eating their meal, Lucy began telling them her experience in Rest Area 10.

"I pulled in there one afternoon to relax. Just to kind of unwind. I had been on a trip following up on interviews for a job."

"What do you do?" asked William.

"Well, at that point I was searching for a teaching job at the collegiate level. I had interviewed at several universities and for some reason just was not satisfied. I learned a long time ago to follow your gut response and just didn't have a positive one, so I was heading back home and came upon Rest Area 10 and decided to pull in and just relax."

Kelly interrupted and apologized. "What did you want to teach?"

"Well, my master's is in philosophy and religion, so something that would be close to that. I was just sort of feeling my way around. I knew I had not arrived there yet but realized I would find it." She smiled. "Or maybe it would find me."

"What happened in Rest Area 10?" asked Maria.

"Well, I pulled in, shut the car off, and got out just to stretch. Just then a highway maintenance truck pulled in."

They all looked at each other.

She noticed and asked if there was something wrong.

William was the first to answer. "No, please continue."

"An older man with long hair got out and grabbed tools out of the back of the truck. You know—rakes and such. He was very polite and said he was there just to tidy up the area a bit. I told him that I was just relaxing from a long drive and a lot of thinking about job hunting. He walked over to a nearby bench, placed his tools against it, and sat down.

"I was just walking around, kind of stretching. He looked up at the sky and said, 'Isn't it a beautiful day out? I had the day off but decided to come out for a little while and work. It just seems to put me in a good mood when I'm here. And sometimes I meet the nicest people that stop.' I looked at him. 'Yes, it's a gorgeous day out.'

"He looked at me in a strange way, not scary strange but a warm and kind way. He asked what kind of a job I was looking for, and I told him that I was at this point unsatisfied with what I had found thus far. He asked why. I told him that so far all the institutions just seemed to want a book-teaching professor. I looked at the worker, laughed a little, and told him that was just not who I was.

"He looked at me again, and I can't explain the feeling I got when he did. It was strange. I mean I had never met this man before, but there was something there. There was something to him. I can't really give you all a good explanation. I just felt that anything he would ask me, I would try to answer. We talked about what I wanted out of a job, what I expected to give, what I expected to receive. I thought at one point that this seemed so much like the interview I wanted to have but never got."

William interrupted her. "What did you want out of an interview, or what were your expectations?"

"I wanted a chance to explain who I was. A chance to explain what I believed in and why. And surprisingly, I was getting more out of a man I had never met, answering questions that were never asked in any previous interview. Strangely, honestly this maintenance worker seemed to possess all the mental and emotional credentials that I had expected to find in previous boards that had interviewed me.

"He told me that maybe I was looking in the wrong place. That maybe I should look at a smaller college, like a private college. I told him that the next college I was to interview with was just that—a small, private, liberal arts college. He asked me the name. I told him it was Culver-Stockton College. That it was in a small town along the Mississippi River. I further explained it was my last stop and I wasn't sure what to do after that if it didn't work out for me. He asked me what my initial thoughts were about this school. I told him I was a little hesitant because of the size of both the town and the school. I thought I would prefer a university in a fairly large town. I guess because I thought more opportunities would exist there."

"How did he respond?" asked Maria.

"His first statement took hold of me, and I thought, *Who is this man?* He said, 'Your opportunities are not born out of what you know or where you think you want to go. Your opportunities are born from your belief in soft whispers of intelligence that touch the most intimate parts of your spirit. They may arrive without your knowledge and will stay until you recognize their value, but I promise you, they will stay.' I looked at him and, without thinking what I was going to say, just said, 'Why would they stay?' He said, 'Because they were created only for you. They have nowhere else to go.' He went on to talk about Culver. He told me he was very familiar with Culver and that he thought it was the perfect place for me. He further described the campus to me and what to expect from the board.

I got the strangest feeling that he knew exactly what he was talking about. In fact, I began to get somewhat excited about my visit there.

"At a very subtle moment in our conversation, I looked up from staring at him and felt perfectly satisfied with accepting a position there if it was offered. In fact, I made a comment to him that if after the interview they offered me a position, I would take it. He looked at me with what I would describe as a fatherly look, a look of confidence in his daughter, and said to me, 'It's the place for you. I just have a feeling they're expecting someone just like you.'

"He went on to explain the campus to me, that it sat on the bluffs above the river, and how beautiful it was. He described it in its seasonal changes. It just sounded so perfect to me. Exactly what I had hoped and prayed to find.

"I stretched a little more, thanked him for his conversation, and told him I'd better get back on the road if I was going to make it to Canton before dark. I got back in my car, rolled the window down to thank him for his advice. He looked at me, again with warm, caring eyes, and told me to enjoy Culver-Stockton. I thanked him again and drove out of Rest Area 10.

"I've never forgotten that experience. I think of it often and have more questions about it than I can find answers. Well, at least till overhearing your conversation."

Kelly looked at Lucy and asked, "So what brought you back here, at this time?"

Lucy looked far away, as if she were trying to bring part of her past into view, and answered, "Well, after hearing what you all said previously about experiences coming out of Rest Area 10, you will all love what I am going to relate."

Maria said, "Please tell us!"

"Well, to shorten this up. I was hired at Culver and have loved every minute I have been there for many reasons. But one night I went to the chapel in the Student Center to get some quiet time and relax. It's a neat little chapel. It's round with beautiful stained-glass windows that run vertically from the floor to the ceiling in four places equally spaced. There's a large round fountain in the center that's about eight feet across that gurgles water the whole time. I fell in love with it the first time I visited there.

"Anyway, this night I went in just to sit and relax and maybe reflect a little on the past. When I did, my memory brought back the man in Rest Area 10. I was just remembering what it felt like being near him and listening to his words. Just then my concentration was broken by someone else coming into the chapel. It wasn't too surprising because lots of people came in there simply to sit and reflect. I nodded a silent hello and went back to my thoughts.

"But the man that came in looked at me and commented, 'This is such a neat place to visit, isn't it? I have always liked the feeling one can get when one comes in here.' I looked at him. 'What do you mean?' He answered, 'When I come in, I feel as though it wraps around me. It envelopes me with something. It's a feeling of compassion, of caring, that is more than just a simple emotional response to the chapel. It's something that invades me. There is something here that makes you feel a part of something. It's a sense of belonging. A sense of being part of something far greater than just yourself. It's a place for someone to talk and someone to listen.' I told him, 'That's why I come in here from time to time after one of my classes. It's a way to reorganize my thoughts.' I looked back to him and paused for a second. I had a fleeting thought, *He looks familiar, or maybe it's just the way he talks.* There was something in his voice. Something I felt more of beyond his words. But I concluded, at least mentally, that it was just the beautiful surroundings and nothing more.

"Bringing me back to the moment, he asked, 'Do you teach here?' I looked at him and did not answer right away. Quickly, he apologized for interrupting my quiet time. But I told him that was fine, and yes, I did teach here. I further explained that I had been there for a few years and how satisfying it was for me. I told him how much I enjoyed the college and the town, that I was glad I had made the decision to interview here, that I felt as though it gave me as much as I gave it, and that I had met some very special friends here.

"He asked me why I chose Culver. I answered that I had made arrangements for an interview and it was my last one of many, but that my decision was helped along by a very nice maintenance worker in a rest area that seemed to have some knowledge of the school and surrounding area. He said, 'It's always good when we receive help at making a decision that may affect the rest of our lives, especially when that help seems to make valid points.' I agreed with him, thanked him for the conversation, but said that I had a dinner date and had to get going. He looked up at me, thanked me also, and told me, 'Have a good evening with fellow professors.'

"I walked out of the chapel, but as I did, I got the strangest feeling that I may have met this man before. And then another thought crossed my mind. *How does he know who I am having dinner with?* I felt compelled to ask him. So I turned to walk back into the chapel, but he was gone. I looked around the tiny room, but there was no one there. He could not have gotten away. There was only one door, and he didn't walk past me.

"But just then, I looked down at the ledge surrounding the fountain and noticed a small object lying there. I walked up, looked down, and picked up a small metal Cross. I turned it around. I noticed something written on it."

Lucy looked at William. "You know what was written on it, don't you?"

He looked at her. "Yes, Rest Area 10."

Meredith and Devon sat in stunned, speechless silence.

Kelly said, "And that's why you came back. That's why you're here."

Maria looked at Lucy. "You now know who the worker is?"

Lucy sat back in her chair and wiped her forehead. "Yes, now there's no doubt. He's the same person that I met in the chapel. And now I know why I came back. I had to be here. I had to overhear your conversations. I had no choice. He brought me here, again."

Kelly looked at Lucy and, with a smile that ran from ear to ear, said, "There's another twist to our story, Lucy."

"What is that?"

"Both sets of my grandparents graduated from Culver."

Devon noticed Meredith's stare at Kelly. "What is it?"

Meredith looked at all of them, sat for a moment in silence, then responded to Devon's question. "He's tying so many things together here. I mean I believe everything everyone has said, but it seems so unbelievable at times."

William said, "It can be difficult at times to fathom why things happen. Why He does what He does and when He does it. But as Maria told you earlier, Meredith, you can find answers to your questions by reading His Word. He stated in one verse that His ways are not our ways, and thankfully, His ways work when ours do not. We can be wrong more times than we are right. Be He, He is never wrong—ever. There is always a purpose to everything He does."

Chapter 14

William looked at Lucy. "Everyone here has had at least one experience in Rest Area 10. Devon and Meredith are the latest. Theirs just happened. Maria and I are somewhat more fortunate, only because we are doctors and have had people come to the ER right out of Rest Area 10." He pointed to Kelly. "Kelly is a doctor as well but had an experience in Rest Area 10 as a small child.

"All of us have been fortunate to have stopped there and to have met the maintenance worker. We all know now how Christ can work, that He is without limitations. For reasons that we will never fully understand, Christ appeared to us all as that worker, and to each of us, He imparted directions to us for our lives. It doesn't really matter what precipitated us pulling in there. It only matters that we did but, more importantly, that it was there for us. That's what our focus should always be on. Not why we pulled in, but that it was there for us when we did.

"Rest Area 10 puts our focus on exactly where it should be, squarely on Christ. As I said, He brings us to Himself. He meets us where He knows it will be comfortable for us. Our entrance to Him, His doorway is small, but all we have to do is walk through it. There will be no bands, no loud noises, no fireworks. But the ground will move and will move our way."

"But," Meredith asked, "how do you hear Him when He speaks to you?"

Maria said, "Meredith, as we move from one experience to another with Him, we develop a way to listen to Him, to hear Him, and it may be quite different from how another may hear His words. One may hear Him speak very audibly while another may just feel His leading while yet another finds His leading in His words from the Bible. But the more we listen, the more we hear, and our lives will prosper."

William looked at the entire group. "Rest Area 10 is quite a place. A lot has happened there over the years, but it's only a start. It's a place of change. It's a place that got our attention. It's a place of refocusing. Our lives do not stay there. He calls us to take His hand and walk toward the direction He moves us, but it will always be with Him. We will never be alone—ever! He has brought us all together to help and encourage each other. To touch each other so that success will be the outcome."

He looked at Devon and Meredith. "Both of you have a chance to build and grow a garden for God. You will start off small and take incremental steps, but as your understanding grows just like your garden, your success in Him will also grow. And from the start, your lives and your garden will touch more lives than you could ever imagine. You will not only supply food for the body. But He will, through you both, also supply food for the soul. Don't worry about what to say or when to say it. He will teach you."

William looked at everyone sitting there, smiled, and continued, "We have all been exactly where you are both at this moment. Those of us that stay here and those that are already here in the community will help you both grow in the Lord." He specifically looked at Meredith. "You may feel as if you left something behind, something that satisfied you, something that satisfied your wants and desires. But what He has shown you here today has more value than everything that is behind you. Your life, and your life with Devon here, has more value not only to you both but also everyone you come into contact with. Please realize that Christ has picked you both for this job, a job of growing food, a job of growing lives."

Meredith teared up slightly and looked at everyone. "I have lived for thirty plus years and was totally unaware of His presence in our lives."

Maria said, "That doesn't matter at all. The good thing is that He was allowing you to move in a certain way, in a certain direction. And that direction was here. Everything you may have thought had meaning and value was simply a way for Him to get you ready for this place, for Rest Area 10."

"But I was so angry at Devon."

"That doesn't matter. It was all part of His plan for you both. He had to get you to a point of acceptance and awareness. He didn't mind how you got there, only that He got you there. Even if it had to be arguing about a future that you were unaware of. He knew your caustic words and acidic attitude would be short-lived. He knew how to correct you both, and for you both, He directly intervened. You both regret now your words to each other, but however awful you may think they were at the time, they did get you to this point. And now because of Him, they are a distant memory. He's telling you to let them go."

Lucy viewed the tiny gathering. "I think I can safely say that not one of us sitting here actually was expecting our entrance and our exit into and from Rest Area 10 to affect our lives as it has."

They all nodded in agreement.

William placed his hands on the table and looked at Devon. "You and Meredith need to find housing for the night and get settled. There's a good motel just down the street run by a great young couple. Tomorrow, after you wake up, we would love to have you out to the house for breakfast so that we can discuss your land purchase and the options that are available here. We will help in any way we can."

Devon was just about to thank everyone for their understanding and their advice, but the noise of sirens outside shattered their tiny gathering. They all turned to see an ambulance and rescue squad vehicle speed by on their way out of town.

William looked at Maria and then to Kelly. "Maybe we should go back to the hospital."

He had no sooner said that than his phone rang. He answered it. "We are on our way." He looked at Maria and Kelly. "There has been an accident out by the curve, and there are fatalities. We need to go." He looked at Devon and Meredith, took a pen out of his pocket, and quickly wrote something on a napkin and handed it to them. "This is my phone number. After you get settled in your motel later today, please call, and we will arrange tomorrow."

He turned to follow Maria and Kelly out the door but stopped and looked back at Lucy, and in the place that Christ often spoke, he heard, "Take Lucy." He looked at her. "You may not understand this, but for a reason beyond me, Christ wants you to go with us."

They made their way out of the cafe to William's car and were quickly on their way back to the hospital.

Maria asked William, "What did the dispatcher say?"

"She said that it appeared a driver crossed the center line of the highway and struck the driver-side door of the oncoming car. Another driver came upon the scene and called in the wreck. She said the drivers of both cars were dead at the scene. The driver of the car that was hit was a woman. I would assume her passenger is her husband. He's unconscious but seems to be without critical injuries."

Kelly interrupted, "Can we pray for them?"

"Absolutely! We will need His assistance," answered Maria.

Kelly began, "Lord, we know You're here and there and with everyone. We just thank You for Your presence and Your help in this matter. Lives have been lost, and we need Your compassion. One is alive, and we pray for Your healing strength in his life. He will need Your courage. We ask this in Your Name as our Lord."

William looked in his rearview mirror at Kelly and thanked her.

Chapter 15

When they arrived at the hospital, they wasted no time in getting parked and getting inside.

They were met by Helen, the ER nurse on duty.

"What's it look like?" asked William.

"Both drivers died at the scene. The passenger in the one car seems to be unhurt, physically anyway, but the driver was his wife."

William took a deep breath and grabbed Maria's hand just as the ambulance and rescue squad arrived. He whispered to her, "Pray for understanding and compassion." He looked at Helen. "Tell the paramedics to bring him to trauma one. We will quickly scrub up and meet them there." He looked at Lucy and politely asked that she stay in the waiting room.

She smiled. "I'll be here."

He touched Kelly's arm. "Please follow us."

She nodded and followed them into scrub.

It didn't take long to scrub and get to trauma unit one.

As they entered the unit, the medics were lifting a man from the gurney to the examining bed. He appeared unconscious.

William asked specifics about the wreck and the deceased.

The medic in charge related the events of the wreck, that the driver that crossed the centerline appeared to be intoxicated. He told

William there was open liquor in the car and the man reeked of alcohol. The woman appeared to have died instantly on impact.

William said, "At this point, autopsies would be irrelevant. I would not authorize them."

The medic said, "I understand, but there will be an investigating officer that needs to question this man. His name is Jim Parker, and his wife was Mary. We will move her body to the morgue."

William simply said, "Thank you."

As the medics left the room, Jim appeared to move a little. William, Maria, and Kelly noticed his movements and stepped closer to him.

He opened his eyes a little and looked around the room. Still dazed and disoriented, he started to speak, but William spoke first.

"Jim, I'm Dr. William Scott. This is my wife, Maria, and friend, Dr. Kelly Brown. I wish we could be meeting under vastly different circumstances." He reached down and softly placed his hand on Jim's arm and started to say more, but Jim started first.

"I know Mary did not make it." He teared up but continued, "I don't really remember what happened, other than we were involved in a wreck. I guess I was knocked unconscious from the impact. But…" He paused, started crying, and raised a hand as if to indicate he wanted to say more.

Maria looked at him. "Jim, we can do this later if you would like."

"No, I need to do this now while it's still fresh in my mind."

Without hesitation, he continued, "At a point past the wreck, I opened my eyes slightly and Mary was being helped out of the car by a man with long hair. I just saw the back of him as he was helping her up. She turned to look at me. I had never seen her so beautiful. She glowed with a light that surrounded her and seemed to run through her. She turned to me and said, 'You're going to be fine. I love you and will never be more than a whisper from you.' I had the very strange feeling of peace and happiness. It was as if I had been on a long trip and was finally home.

"The man helping her turned to me, and I saw His face. I knew Who it was, and with the most inspiring eyes I have ever seen, He spoke to me, saying, 'You are never alone—ever! If sadness creeps in, just remember this moment. Remember Mary as she is at this moment because this is who she will always be. Remember what I say to you. My voice is your strength and a road to your understanding. I am with you always. From this moment on, your life will never be without love and will never be without us.' They turned and walked into the rest area, and I passed out." He wiped his tears away with a hand and continued, "There is more. I need something from you."

He looked at them, and William said, "Anything, Jim."

"I just need to talk, and I need you to listen. For a reason beyond my thinking, I know you will understand what I am about to say. There is more to this, to what happened. Some of it makes sense to me, but some of it I question. Some of it I ask why. Maybe there are no answers right now. Maybe you will not fully understand what I am about to say. But as Mary and Christ were walking into the rest area, He kept talking to me. Or at least I was hearing His voice somewhere inside of me. He told me that this place, this rest area, was not a place of endings but a place of beginnings. A new start. A start with more answers than questions. A place to solve problems. He said, 'I brought you here. There is more value in this curve and this rest area than you are aware of, but in the days beyond today, you will understand because I promise I will teach you.'"

He looked at all of them again. "I don't understand my strength at this point, but my weakness was absorbed by what He spoke to me. I felt as if I was flying, as if everything that could drag me down was left far below me. I felt as if I was taken away from harm, from debilitating sadness.

"I felt as if He, as if Christ was taking me away from my emotions of loss to a heart filled with freedom. A freedom away from everything that would take me down, that could destroy me. At that moment, I believe that what He told me is what He is about. He can take us away from everything that works against us. And He replaces it with something pure, something strong, something that will last forever. Something permanent. And it can come from no one else. There is nothing in life that can replace it, nothing that can fill us up the way He can.

"I did not feel as if I had lost Mary. I felt as if I had absorbed her, as if she was now a part of me. And the greatest thing I felt was I would never experience an aloneness that is associated with her death. I would feel sadness at her loss, but I would never feel alone."

The professionalism that all three doctors had exhibited prior to Jim's speaking was slowly melting away. All three became teary-eyed.

Kelly touched Jim's arm as her emotions spilled over. "I cannot fully understand your pain at this moment, but I do understand Rest Area 10. My life changed there as well." She smiled teary eyes at him and squeezed his arm.

He looked off into the space of the room, gathered his thoughts, and asked, "Can I see my wife's body?"

William spoke first. "Yes, we can take you to her, but first allow us to do a quick examination of you. I just want to make sure you're as well as you appear to be."

Jim nodded. "Okay."

Maria grabbed another pillow from the closet and placed it under Jim's head. "Just close your eyes, Jim. Try to relax and tell me if anything hurts where I am touching you. I will lift your arms and legs and maneuver them a little." She gently explored his body with her hands and was pleased that everywhere she put pressure he felt no pain.

"Remarkably, I feel fine. I have no pain, at least physical."

William looked at Kelly. "Could you go out and get us a wheelchair?"

"Sure. I'll be right back."

William walked close to the bed. "Let's get you up, but just to where you are sitting on the edge of the bed. Then we'll see how you feel. It may take a few minutes, but we will help you get into the wheelchair."

"Thank you."

William and Maria got on opposite sides of him, gently reached under his arms and around his back. They got him up slowly to the edge of the bed and let him hang his legs off the side.

"How does that feel?" asked Maria.

He smiled at them. "I feel okay."

Just then Kelly came in with a wheelchair and pushed it next to the bed.

Jim looked at them. "I think I can walk."

"I know you probably can," said William, "but hospital protocol requires us to put you in a wheelchair while you're here."

"I understand."

While Kelly held the chair, William and Maria slowly got Jim off the bed and into the chair.

"The morgue is not far. I'll take you down," said William.

Jim nodded and relaxed in the chair.

As William began pushing him out of the room and into the hallway, Jim turned and asked Maria and Kelly to please accompany him and William.

"This is a point I did not expect would ever happen, at least this soon or under these circumstances. And even with the events I described, I don't want to be alone."

Maria looked down at him. "Then you won't be. We will be by your side."

Jim turned his head toward Maria and Kelly. He raised his right hand as if to say stop. He said, "There is something else. Something I just remembered. Something that Christ said to me. He said there would be four. I didn't attach any meaning to it until right now."

"What is it?" asked Kelly.

"It meant I would be surrounded by four people, and there are only three of you. There has to be someone else."

He looked at them questioningly. They all looked at each other.

William thought, *Of course, Lucy. That's why he brought her. There's a connection here.* He didn't know what it was, but Christ did. He looked at the group. "I'll be right back."

He left to go get Lucy from the waiting room. As he entered, he found her quietly sitting in a chair.

She looked up at him, and he looked down at her.

"I have a sinking feeling, William, I'm somehow connected here to the affected people. I don't know how, but as I was praying for the situation, Christ told me He would give me the strength I would need."

William nodded and simply asked her to follow him. They walked through the doors and into the hallway. She could see Maria and Kelly standing beside a wheelchair that obviously had a man sitting in it.

As they got closer, Jim turned to William and Lucy. He could not contain his emotions. He burst into tears.

Lucy screamed, "Oh, my God, *no!* No, Jim! Not Mary! Please not Mary! Please, Lord, not Mary."

He tried to stand. Maria and Kelly each grabbed an arm and held him up as Lucy ran into his arms crying uncontrollably.

Lucy kept sobbing and saying, "No, Jim. Not Mary. Please not Mary."

She buried her head in his neck. He placed a hand on the back of it. "It will be all right, Lucy. It will be all right. Let me sit down. I'm feeling weak."

She let go of him, and he sat back in the wheelchair.

Lucy knelt in front of him, crying, and placed her hands on his knees.

He picked both up, gripped them tightly, looked in her tear-filled eyes, and took a deep breath. "I need to tell you something. It will help. I promise it will help you understand." He looked up at William, Maria, and Kelly, who had questions written all over their faces. He teared up slightly again. "Lucy is Mary's best friend. We all teach at the same college."

William reached for Maria's hand. He placed his other hand on Kelly's shoulder. This was a moment where all five realized the power of Christ. It was a power that never left one alone to face anything by oneself. His strength was there. His wisdom would lead not only their thoughts but also their words. This was a journey unexpected by everyone that stood in the hallway, but it was becoming clear that it was a journey that had to happen and that Christ was right among them.

Jim looked at Lucy with tears streaming down her face.

She said, "I am so sorry. So, so sorry."

In a calming voice he said, "It's okay, Lucy. It will be okay. I need to tell you what happened. I mean right after the wreck. It will make you feel better. It won't take away your pain, but it will help to heal your loss." He reached over, wiped her tears away, placed a hand on either side of her face, and looked into her eyes. "It will be okay." He then began relating to her what had happened right after the wreck.

After he finished, he looked at them all. "I haven't told any of you this, but about twenty minutes before the wreck, Mary wanted to drive. I thought it was kind of strange, but she looked at me and said, 'I need to drive.' She saved my life. My life had to continue. Hers did not. I don't understand some things in life and the reason Christ allows them to happen, but I do understand this. I may not like it. It may tear me apart for a time, but I know His reasons far outdistance my own."

He looked into Lucy's face and continued, "We can't see into tomorrow. We don't have His vision. We lack so many things in understanding His ways, but He has given us one thing. It's the greatest thing any of us could ever receive. Through our faith, He gives us life. And that life, the one that He gave us through His sacrifice, will never end. Mary's not here. That part of her, that physical sense that we will miss, desperately at times, is gone. But what we loved in her, that person that Christ made, will only be a whisper away. At the rest area, He promised us that. Those were His words." With tears streaming down his face, Jim finished. "And we know He always fulfills His promises to us, always!" He looked at Lucy, then to the rest of the group. "Let's go say goodbye to Mary."

Chapter 16

Lucy stood up, stepped to the side of Jim's wheelchair, but held on to his left hand. It was a short walk to the morgue.

As they arrived at the door, William stopped pushing the chair and walked in front of Jim. "Could I pray for all of us before we go in?"

"Yes. Please do."

They all bowed their heads, and in a solemn voice William began.

"Lord, we don't understand some things in life that can tear at our hearts, but we thank You for allowing Jim to see You, to hear Your voice, and to feel the love You have for him. We thank You for who You are and that we can find courage in You. We thank You for Mary's life and fully realize she stands next to You, wrapped in more love and happiness than any of us could ever give another. We thank You for the cleansing power of Your blood and Your promise of life everlasting."

William returned to his placed behind the wheelchair.

Maria reached over, placed a hand on top of William's resting on the handles of the wheelchair. With her free hand she took hold of Kelly's right hand and nodded as if to say they were ready.

Jim looked up at Lucy. "This will be all right, Lucy. Remember what Mary said. What she told me at Rest Area 10 was not only for me, but it was for you as well. Through Christ, she knew you would be here. Christ knew we would need each other. Remember what He said. We, you and I, are letting go of something here. But it's only the physical side of Mary, not the heart side of her. Not the love side of her. We may fall apart, and that's all right. She meant more to us than most things in life, but we are allowing Him to take our loss and turn it into something that will strengthen us both."

As they entered the small room, Mary's body was lying on a gurney with only her face exposed.

Lucy began crying again and tried to speak but couldn't.

Jim tightened his grip on Lucy's hands and comforted her by saying, "We are here not to let go of what we have loved. We will never have to do that. We are never required to give up love. We are simply acknowledging that love and thanking our Lord for blessing our lives with her. She changed us, Lucy. She came to you and me in the moment we needed what she could give us, and for reasons unknown to you and me, this was the time Mary had to go home. We both, you and I, are torn apart by what we see lying on the table, as we should be. Our hearts are broken, torn in two. We feel lost, but this will all pass.

"That moment in Rest Area 10, when Mary and Christ spoke to me, my life and all that ever meant anything to me in my life was reborn. We will rise above our pain and our loss because there is no end here. Nothing that is connected to Him or to us through Mary will ever end.

"This is a moment of grief, but it is also a moment when all that ever matters in our lives will consume us. His love for us, and the way He stands by us, in this moment, must be our focus. Our grief and our disbelief in what happened will pass." He looked up at Lucy. "We will be okay, Lucy. He will take care of us. He's given us a window into each other. A window that will enable us to see what we need to see and a road that will take us there." He squeezed her hand, turned, and looked at William. "I need your help."

"Anything."

"Mary wanted to be cremated with her ashes scattered on that part of campus that overlooks the river. Can you arrange with a local funeral home to have the cremation done?"

William reached over and placed a hand on Jim's shoulder. "I will get the necessary paperwork done and make the contact. I would like to admit you for the night, just for observation."

Lucy asked, "Would it be a problem if I stayed with Jim?"

"Not at all. We'll take care of it."

William looked at Maria and Kelly. "We'll go make preparations for your admittance and give you two time alone. We'll be back to get you in fifteen or twenty minutes."

Jim looked away from them to Mary's body, then back to the group. "Thank you."

William, Maria, and Kelly left the morgue.

Jim looked back to Mary's body, kept a tight grip on Lucy's hand, and wept.

Lucy knelt beside Jim's wheelchair, placed her head on the armrest, and cried.

This was a moment of release, a moment when all that was lost in Mary was realized. The weight of this moment, of Mary's loss, pushed the emotions of both Jim and Lucy to the bottom of life's expectations.

Lucy raised her head up and looked into Jim's tear-filled eyes, but nothing needed to be said. This was a moment when silence was the only answer, when faith was the only solution.

From somewhere inside them both, from a hidden place, a place in which both were now existing suspended only by their friendship and love for Mary, a voice was heard by both.

With unmistakable resonance and clarity, Christ spoke to them. "Death leads to life. It always has and always will. Trust in me and what I have said. You will both be reborn away from the grief you are now consumed by."

The tiny room that seemed only to demonstrate death was now filled with life.

Chapter 17

Jim looked up at Lucy. "Did you just hear what I did, that we are to trust Him, that we will be reborn away from our grief?"

"Yes, I heard His words as well."

Jim looked beyond the space that was this room to the greater world that lay before them, to an unknown area of new thoughts, new reasons to live and to prosper. He looked up to Lucy. "We walk away from here leaving nothing behind, leaving nothing that attaches us to the pain of loss. We simply walk away."

There was a slight knock on the morgue door; and William, Maria, and Kelly came back in.

William looked at them both. "Everything is set for your stay overnight. We will help you get to a room and get settled in. When it's convenient, there are the necessary papers to fill out, but there's no hurry."

Jim thanked them for their help. "I'm ready to go."

Lucy grabbed his hand. "I will stay with you and help get things in order."

Jim looked up at Lucy and smiled. "Once I get settled in a room, can we spend the rest of the day remembering Mary?"

Lucy returned his smile. "Absolutely."

Jim looked to William. "I want to thank you for your help and understanding. It means a great deal to me. I could never repay you all for your heartfelt outreach."

Maria said, "That's why we're here, Jim. If it would help, we can take things from your car and hold them till you decide what to do."

"I would appreciate that. I will probably need the registration and insurance card from the glove box. Our luggage is in the trunk. Would it be possible for you to get it and also bring it here?"

Lucy interrupted, "We can put it in my car once I get it here."

"If you would like, we can take you back to your car at the restaurant," said William.

Lucy said, "Can we get Jim settled in his room first? Then can I ride back with you to the restaurant, get my car, and go to where Jim's car was towed?"

William looked at both Lucy and Jim. "Anything you want. We will help in any way we can."

Jim looked away from the group, as if lost in the moment. A tear ran from his right eye down his cheek.

Lucy firmly held his hand. "What is it, Jim?"

He looked at William and answered Lucy's question. "I know this may seem out of the ordinary, but where are Mary's clothes she was wearing at the time of the accident?"

Maria said, "The nursing staff in the ER will have them."

"Could I have them brought to my room, please?"

Maria smiled slightly. "I will get them now for you."

He looked up at Maria and thanked her. "I need something tangible right now. Something that is Mary. Something to hang on to. The clothes, in their own way, will enable me to grab on to her."

"We understand," said William.

Maria turned to get the clothes as they made their way to the elevator and Jim's room.

This was a time that would go by, moment by moment. Each slow step and each small thought would lead to the past with revelations of the future. Jim and Lucy would be moving from what they knew to what they did not, but their extreme sadness and consuming grief would be absorbed by the visions Jim saw and the words that touched his ears and his heart.

As they entered the elevator, Lucy kept a grasp on Jim's hand. The doors closed, and silence filled the tiny cubicle. As quickly as it started, it stopped, and the doors opened.

William motioned to the right. "Your room is just two doors down. It's 110."

He looked at Kelly and asked her to please get the door.

The room was like any other hospital room—a bed, a stand for a food tray, and two chairs.

Jim looked to William. "If it's okay, I would just prefer to sit in the chair."

"That's fine."

Lucy kept hold of Jim's right hand, and Kelly stepped up to help get him from the wheelchair to the room's chair.

After they got him in place and comfortable, Lucy let go of Jim's hand. "Could I get a ride back to the restaurant with you and get my car?"

"Absolutely," answered William.

She looked down at Jim. "I will be right back."

Jim nodded and looked off into the pain that enveloped his moment.

Just then Maria came back into the room with Mary's clothes all neatly folded and laid them on Jim's lap. She smiled down at him. "If there is anything you need at any time, please call us."

Jim smiled. "Thank you."

Lucy again smiled down at him. "I'll get my car and be right back."

As they left Jim's room, Lucy began to cry again. She looked at them. "I've lost my best friend, and so has Jim."

Kelly reached over and grabbed Lucy's arm. "Christ never leaves us alone. He understands exactly what you are going through and exactly what you are feeling."

"Thank you. I know He does."

They made their way out of the hospital to William's car. He opened the rear door for Lucy and reiterated that anything she needed they would see she got.

She smiled back at him and sat down in the back seat.

It was a short ride back to the restaurant and Lucy's car. As they pulled into the parking lot, William gave Lucy instructions on where the lot was that they had towed Jim's car.

As she got out of the car, Maria said, "If there's anything either of you need, just let us know."

"I will." She paused and then continued with a tear-filled smile, "Thank you very much for being the kind of people you are. Can I give you a call tonight and maybe grab a bite to eat or—"

She didn't finish her statement as William said, "Call us when you want to, and we'll come by and pick you up."

Lucy whispered, "Thank you," and walked to her car.

As William drove from the restaurant toward home, he looked over at Maria. "They will need our prayers and whatever strength we can give them through our Lord."

Maria looked at Kelly sitting in the back seat. "Maybe you and I can fix dinner tonight for Lucy. We will offer to have Jim come with her, but something tells me he may want to stay at the hospital."

"I'll help in any way I can."

Chapter 18

Lucy pulled out of the restaurant parking lot and headed toward the lot where Jim's car was towed.

She was apprehensive about seeing it. It would be a place of death as some might see it. She was having a surge of emotions that ran from her fingertips to her feet. They were not bad, just very intense. They seemed to invade her body from somewhere. As they slowly enveloped her, a strange yet familiar feeling gently swept over her. It was a warm, comforting wind that soothed her thoughts, and for an instant, she was momentarily viewing the old gentleman in the chapel at Culver. It was an intense sense of peace, a mental scene of serenity. He spoke no words, offered no thoughts, but there was a language that she heard. From here, she was guided away from the desperation of loss that accompanies death to a place of perfect peace where darkness is consumed by light and life moves on.

And from the depths of her searching came four simple words spoken by a voice of power that pushed itself into her. It was strong yet yielding to her understanding. She heard, "Life is never-ending."

It gently and silently moved her away from tears to a sense of light, a sense of peace.

She pulled into the lot, stopped her car, and bowed her head. In closing her eyes, she asked for strength and courage.

As she raised her head, a man appeared from a small building just inside the lot.

He walked to her car. "Can I help you?"

"Yes, I'm here to get the belongings out of the Parker car. Can you take me to it?"

The man pointed to a green Hyundai. "It's the Hyundai over there."

Lucy nodded and smiled a soft thank you.

She pulled her car up next to Mary's.

She turned her car off and sat there looking at the crumpled-up green Hyundai. She sat motionless, unable to move. There was something going through her. At one point it gripped her, tearing at her emotions. It ripped away at her thoughts of her future or at least what she had envisioned her future to be. Tears ran from her eyes to her cheeks. The wreck had destroyed the car, but it also had taken from her, her best friend. It took away all of the future conversations they might have had. It ended the evenings of walking together across campus. It was how she and Mary would sometimes solve problems. Their walks together by themselves or sometimes with Jim were cathartic. Campus in the evening, looking at the Mississippi below, somehow offered a way to lift oneself above one's problems to where solutions sometimes resided. It was a place of peace, a place of soft sounds rarely interrupted by the outside world. It was here, on the green lawn in summer and snow-covered ground in winter, that she and Mary developed an understanding of each other and the Lord that directed their steps. Their intense conversations provided a way to explore their lives, to develop their questions for each other, and ultimately to work through with each other's help possible solutions.

She was not here. She was not sitting looking at a wrecked car. Her mind, heart, and soul were bound to whatever energy provided her strength, to return to the college and the Missouri hills it was built upon. Her thoughts raced through the years of the past, of places they had been and discoveries they had made as friends.

This was a walk she had to take, a painful disturbance in her life. It had to be addressed. It had to be confronted. It was an experience that, at first, must be internalized. In her thoughts, as she understood them to be, she would allow Mary's death to consume her. All the good, bad, and indifferent aspects of loss would be allowed to bombard her. It would take its toll on her. She knew that, but she also knew that no matter what depth she might sink to, there was always a way out, always Someone to lean upon for strength and courage. He, Christ, would always be with her.

She knew that her acceptance of Mary's death would be the moment when healing would begin to occur. And the beginning was now.

The first step out of her car to Mary's would be the beginning. And the more steps she made away from the car and death would be steps to a renewed sense of living and life.

She raised her head; opened her eyes; and, in a soft voice that no one could hear, whispered, "I will miss you."

Lucy walked hesitantly to the car, stopped and started, prayed for strength, and finally walked up to the car.

She put her hands on the top above the driver side, the point of impact. She sighed, closed her eyes to what she saw.

Memories raced through her mind of the car on campus or seeing it go by and waving to Mary. She teared up again, knowing that she would no longer see that. It was slipping into history. *But all things do*, she thought.

She reached in and got the keys off the dash. She walked to the rear of the car, opened the trunk lid, and unloaded their luggage and their emergency things such as blankets and extra water. She emptied the trunk and placed it all in her car.

She placed the keys back on the dash of the car, minus Jim's and Mary's house keys. She also opened the glove box and center console and grabbed all the contents there as well.

Walking back to her car, she sat down and placed what she had in her hand on her passenger seat.

But as she was about to close the door and leave, she had a strange thought, a mental picture.

She saw a small book under the driver side seat of their car. She shook her head as if to say, "It's nothing." But there was a persistent pulling of her. Or was it a pushing? Whatever it was, she could not ignore it.

She got out of her car, walked back to the other car, opened the back door, and looked under the front seat.

A chill ran through her. There was a small black leather book tucked neatly under the seat.

She reached in, grabbed it, and pulled it into view. It was a small Bible with Jim's and Mary's names embossed on the cover in gold letters.

She felt compelled to open it up, but she stopped and wondered if she should.

No, she thought. She had to.

She opened the cover to the first page. She recognized Mary's writing.

Clearly and concisely written were the words, "Our Emergency Kit—It's all we need."

Lucy began to cry again. She remembered how Mary was never shy about sharing her faith, and that was always forefront in both Jim's and Mary's thoughts.

She turned the first page and found a few pieces of folded paper with writing on them. She picked them up, opened them, and began reading.

> Whoever may find this, know that our life together was lived in accordance with Christ's words and how we, Jim and I, perceived our direction should go. Neither of us wanted anything more than to do what Christ wanted us to do.
>
> We had our share of ups and downs, of successes and failures, but we never lost sight of Him in our everyday lives. We always believed His words and lived His promises to us every day.
>
> We are thankful to have had the walk we have had, to touch so many lives and to be touched by so many lives.

She shuffled the papers and found one with her name on it. She read aloud,

> To my friend Lucy, Christ provided such a special person in you. Thank you for opening your life up to me, for allowing me to be part of your life experience. It has changed mine.
>
> If we can somehow explore our life through the intervention of another's life, then we have found meaning not only in ours but also the other person's. You helped guide me to a beautiful experience that I would have otherwise

missed. Your life has meant as much to me as it
has to you.

The words on the paper became blurred from the tears filling Lucy's eyes. These were heartfelt thoughts that were exposed to anyone who might have found them.

She thought, *I will stop reading for now. It feels like Jim should be included in this.*

She placed the paper back in the Bible, walked back to her car, and left for the hospital.

Chapter 19

Alone with only his thoughts, Jim's mind was a torrent of grief racing through memories in a place he did not want to be, at a time in his life he could never have envisioned him being.

He brought the entire bundle of Mary's folded clothes to his face, inhaled the smells that were only hers, and wept.

The weakness of his human side slowly took hold of him, and his loss consumed him. *How can I move forward?* he thought.

As he sat there in that cold hospital room, absolutely empty and void of all that had mattered to him in his life, his aloneness overtook him. His tears became deep, guttural moans of loss.

He asked in a weak voice, "How can I go on? How can my life have any meaning to me now? I have lost everything that mattered to me. Which way do I turn?"

These questions were overtaken by his emotions. He knew where his beliefs were. He knew what he had seen in Rest Area 10. He knew what he had heard there as well. He knew his faith would take him where he needed to go.

But at this moment, at this exact space in time, his physical loss controlled his thoughts. He knew this would pass. It would take time, but it would pass.

He held Mary's clothes to his face again and buried his tears in the folds of her red flannel shirt.

In a weak voice, he whispered to the ears of one that could hear. "I will miss more of you than I can ever realize at this moment."

His tears soaked Mary's shirt, but beyond the emptiness of this room and his heart, a soft thought of love slid into his being. He could feel its warmth. It was a touch of Mary, a simple but invading touch. It was as if her hands were upon his shoulders and her love spoke to his heart. It was not an audible set of words, a sentence as one would hear, but nonetheless she was touching him. The energy that once flowed through Mary, that essence that was who she was and still was, wrapped around him and ran through him. He knew he was not alone.

His loss would want to grip his emotions and his life. It would want to steal his understanding that simply stood at the doorstep of his life, but he would not allow his senses to be stolen from him. He would not allow his faith to lose to his loss. His faith would push all that tried to consume him to the side, and the power that could be found in Christ's words would prevail.

The beautiful woman he saw being helped from the car and her voice would permeate his thoughts, and her words would eventually overcome all that tried to steal his strength. In this moment, the tragic events that lay before him would not win.

He closed his eyes to that darkness that tried to fill his heart, bowed his head into Mary's clothes, and spoke to all that stood just out of eyesight, that waited just beyond the horizon.

In a voice, with emotions that could be heard by only those that waited in the light, he spoke to an unseen Mary.

"I am alone but do not feel lonely. This may be painful, but I am not in pain. My loss may try to grip me, but I will not lose my grip on the Cross and what I shared with you. No other one can lessen or steal that from me. No one!"

He would speak no other words. All those that were there, at that exact moment, would take the coldness of loss and cast it to the unknown. The silence of love would be all that he needed. He cried once again into her clothes.

But from a memory of a small chapel, on a small college campus, a whisper slid across his senses. It was not heard by his ears or seen by his eyes, but it did softly roll into him. It took hold of him.

All that he was and all that brought him to this point opened him up and pulled out the emptiness of loss and filled every corner of his being with love. It ran like water into him. No space was left untouched by this power. It covered and consumed all that tried to break him.

He sat back in his chair, with Mary's clothes still on his lap, took a deep breath, closed his eyes, and slowly slipped into sleep.

Chapter 20

Lucy's drive back to the hospital was just that, a drive.

Her mind floated between the past and the present, between what she thought and what she had read on the paper. It was not a predetermined set of thoughts. It was not rational. It was just a wandering of ideas of what was and what might be. It was a journey into an unknown piece of land. A journey we all must make but few of us really believe we will experience.

The day hit her like a blast. It took her breath away and momentarily left her speechless.

She reached up, wiped her eyes, and mentally told herself she would need to regain some composure to prop up Jim.

She pulled into the hospital parking lot, shut her car off, and simply sat. Bowing her head, she spoke a short prayer for strength, a prayer for guidance.

She got out and walked to the doors while thinking, *Can I run from all of this? Can I turn my back on this and leave? Can I run away from the pain that consumes me?*

The answer was easy: keep walking.

And from a soft touch that few could hear or even believe, she felt a gentle nudge, a grasp of hands guiding her into the next moment, into her next movement.

She whispered as she walked through the doors, "Thank You, Lord."

The short walk to Jim's room was tearful for her, but it was one of listening and one of believing that the words that would touch her lips would be chosen not from her depths of grief but from the heights of her faith.

She moved toward the door of his room. She stopped, took a deep breath, slowly opened the door, and walked in.

He was asleep in the chair with Mary's clothes on his lap.

Lucy would not wake him. She would allow him to sleep.

She thought, *I don't know where he is right now. I don't know where his thoughts are leading him or the land he is now walking in. I will not disturb that.*

She sat down in a chair next to his, placed the Bible on her lap, and closed her eyes.

Chapter 21

Jim's eyes slowly opened. He looked at Lucy sitting in the other chair. She was awake. She smiled slightly and started to say something, but he raised his hand as if to say, "Wait."

Instead, he began, "I cried into Mary's clothes. I guess, basically crying myself to sleep." He paused and looked at the clothes resting on his lap. "She would not want us to be consumed by this."

He smiled at Lucy and reached for her hand. He held it between both of his. "We both know she would want us to celebrate her life and her first few moments with Christ. Her radiance was written all over her face, Lucy. She was not sad. She was beautiful. Christ's love radiated from her and pierced every fiber of my being. It took hold of me, Lucy. It gripped me."

He paused and looked out the window, then back to Lucy. "We cannot stop the movement of this day. The sun will rise and make its trek across a cloudless sky or a sky filled with thunderstorms. It may be a day of heat or a day of freezing winds. But it will be a day of change. It will always be a day of change. Change is a recurring theme found in nature, and we are a part of that. Mary was a part of that. It's a life-and-death process for the moment and the foreseeable future. We have not come to change this, Lucy. We simply have come to understand when and why change occurs and how to live with that change."

He looked down at Mary's clothes again and back to Lucy. "We are going to be fine. We will move through this. There is a purpose to this. The change will be good for us. Otherwise, Mary would never have been called home. I will forever see them as Christ helped her from the car. I will see their faces and the smiles that were given to me to help with my understanding. They were powerful and potent. They fed an area in my spirit that was starving. In my life, those faces and smiles will never be forgotten."

He looked at the Bible on Lucy's lap. "I'm glad you found that. It had completely slipped my mind." He had a hint of a laugh. "Mary and I worked on that one night many years ago. She insisted we do something with our Bible and that we leave it in our car in case anything should ever happen to one or both of us. She was always thinking of the what-ifs. I agreed with her, and we sat down and wrote our thoughts to each other should one of us die before the other or should an unsuspecting person find it."

Lucy handed it to Jim. "I read the note she wrote to me. I have felt the same way about her the moment I met her. She made my life at Culver an amazing experience."

Jim interrupted her. "You were both good for each other. She really needed you at times when a woman's perspective was necessary. You were able to provide things to her that I could not, but your experiences with her benefited me just as much. Because of some of your discussions, she and I were able to look deeper into each other and our relationship."

He took the Bible, laid it on top of Mary's clothes that were still on his lap, and opened it. He took the folded paper out that said, "To Jim, my friend," and unfolded it. He looked at Lucy and asked, "Can I read Mary's words to you?"

"Please do."

He began reading.

> I'm not sure what has or has not happened. I don't know how my thoughts will find you. I'm not sure if you're reading them now or an unsuspecting traveler is reading them. I think it was only necessary that I write them down, with a prayer, that you would be the reader.
>
> I could write pages describing my thoughts on you and how you have affected my life.
>
> But I don't think I need to. I believe only a few words can explain my attachment to you, to our life together.
>
> Your greatest asset, the quality that most endeared you to me, was your ability to share your vulnerability with me. That will always be your greatest strength and your greatest asset.
>
> I have often thought how funny it may seem that we could find strength in the other's weakness. It was like a vessel full of life-giving water. Each time we poured it out to the other, we both benefited, and our vessels always stayed full. Neither of us ever felt empty, alone, or afraid. As Christ fed us, we shared those meals with each other.
>
> My dearest Jim, we never felt hungry with each other. When we decided that fasting should be an integral aspect of our weekly routine, I will never forget your one-sentence thought: "Fasting is not about giving up food. It's about being fed."

Jim looked up and away from Mary's words. He looked straight ahead, but what he saw was not the stark walls of his hospital room. He saw a young and beautiful Mary walking across a campus, a campus that they had built their lives around, a place they had built their thoughts upon.

It was a place where they had taught, but it was also a place they had become students to each other's own desires in life and how to meet those desires and how to accomplish their shared goals.

This is what he saw. This is what she had given him.

He looked back to Lucy with tear-filled eyes and responded to Mary's words.

"I never wanted to be away from her, away from her thoughts that gave birth to my own. She made me think. We explored things together. I could have never arrived at the conclusions I did on so many things without her input. She always kept things moving in a good direction, and there was always a destination. And it was always a good place to find and to be."

Lucy sat quietly. She did not want to interrupt his thoughts or his emotional travels that consumed him at this moment. It was a place Mary's words had taken him, a place he had to go. From beyond the world neither of them could see yet knew to exist, Mary was speaking to him, and he was listening.

He looked at Lucy and smiled. "You know we were in a perfect place. I mean at Culver. We were given an opportunity." He stopped, shook his head as a tear rolled down his right cheek, and continued, "We were so fortunate to experience each other in that setting. We got to live each other's moments in a way that could only have been lived there. Our lives had to occur there. We had to confront life there, together."

Lucy interrupted Jim. "You know it was preparing you. Mary's life was preparing you, and me to a degree, for what was and is coming. Grief makes it a mystery right now. I mean where we are going and how we are to get there. But you and I both know there is a road ahead of us." She looked at him, right into his eyes. "We both know and believe that Christ does not leave loose ends. We may not like how He moves our lives around, and at times we may feel as though we are being blown around like a leaf in a strong wind. But there is always a reason, and it's the right reason."

Jim smiled at her. "You're exactly right. We have to move forward. We have to let go of some things about Mary, but we will always hold tight to those things that can carry us along unencumbered by her death."

He looked away again and continued, "But at this moment, I am simply human. I hurt from a place I have never been before. I feel lost, walking aimlessly, trying to find my loss, but knowing I never will. I am in the bottom of a waterless well able only to see the light from above but with no way to get to the top. My grief consumes me." He wiped the tears from his eyes, looked at Lucy, and sat quietly.

Lucy walked close to him, placed her hands on his shoulders, and squeezed them tightly.

He looked up at her. "Why don't you go out to eat with William, Maria, and Kelly? I think I need to just have some alone time, read more of her words to me, and just try to adjust somewhat to what may be ahead of me. I'll be fine. We both know I'm not alone." He smiled at her again. "You go ahead, but when you're finished, I need your company to get me through this night."

She squeezed his shoulders again. "I will be back after supper." She turned, left his room for the hallway and to her own tears. She stood quietly with her back against the wall and cried.

Chapter 22

William, Maria, and Kelly were waiting in the car as Lucy walked from the hospital.

She opened up the passenger side rear door and slid in. She looked at them all. "This is not at all what I had anticipated when I was on my way back here. I guess I knew there was a reason why He brought me here, but it was simply that I had to return."

Kelly, sitting in the other back seat, reached over, and placed a hand on Lucy's arm. She gave Lucy a warm, compassionate look. "Many times our faith is the only thing that leads us and the only thing that keeps us going. It's the only thing that can provide us the answers we need."

Lucy looked at her, then up to William and Maria, who had turned around. "Today, yesterday, and tomorrow are all part of what is going on here. We may not agree with what is happening, but it is Christ's doing. And for every problem we think we are facing He does have an answer."

"Yes, He does," said William.

Lucy exhaled a heavy breath and looked out her window. "I'm ready."

From out of nowhere, Kelly spoke. "There will always be a beautiful sunrise that leads to a day of surprises, that leads to a soothing sunset. The darkness may overtake us, but there will always be another sunrise."

William looked in the mirror to the back seat and said, "Always." He paused. "If it's okay with all of you, I thought we may go to the Square for supper. It's a small restaurant with an organic menu. It's always a quiet place to enjoy one's company. They have little rooms that only sit a few people, and right now, Maria and I think that it would be good for all of us to be off together."

Lucy said, "That sounds fine with me."

They had not driven very far when William turned toward an older-looking building. It was obviously an old business whose structure someone had rejuvenated. It was two stories of brick with large open windows across the front and the second story. The windows were trimmed with wood, giving the building an older appearance of something from the past. Something built to last the ravages of time and exposure. It seemed to Lucy it was appropriately named the Square.

William pulled his car into the lot and parked. He turned to look at Lucy. "We have a small private room inside. I think you'll like it."

She smiled, and they all got out of the car and headed in. The hostess greeted them and ushered them to the small room with only one table that seated around six people. She took their drink orders and motioned to the menus that were already on the table. They spread out around the wooden table and sat down.

William looked at Lucy. "We are here to help, Lucy. If you want to talk a little or simply sit in silence, we are fine with whatever you want."

Lucy looked at all of them and chose her words carefully. "Mary was a friend like no other." She sat back in her chair, reached back into her memory, and began sharing her thoughts with them. "I met them my very first day at Culver. As I was carrying my boxes to my office, they saw me and asked if they could help. They introduced themselves. We talked the whole time as we carried boxes and unloaded them. It was an exchange quite like the exchange I talked about having in Rest Area 10 with the old maintenance worker. It was not a conversation that had to be pushed or pulled a certain way. It simply flowed and moved in a direction, that to me, seemed to be predetermined. We talked the whole time about Culver and what I should expect and what I hoped for."

She rested, closing her eyes, and then reopened them. "Jim and Mary had been there for a few years. Our conversation gave me a sense of being in the right place at the right time. I kept thinking about what the worker from the rest area had said, something to the fact that Culver would be my last stop.

"It was late in the afternoon. I had not found housing yet, but I did have a motel room for the night. I told them that, and they invited me to their house for supper. I was kind of relieved for that. The afternoon of conversation turned into a night of conversation. I shared stories of growing up and of dreams I had for my life, and they shared theirs. I became tired, thanked them for their hospitality and help, and went to my motel room. But I lay in bed for the longest time thinking about them. Several times during our conversations we discussed our belief systems and how Christ played a big role in the movement of our lives. As I fell asleep, I thanked Him for the day and also for Jim and Mary."

The sense of the moment was broken by their waitress coming to take orders and setting their drinks down.

William motioned to Lucy, "You first."

She smiled and ordered, then Kelly, Maria, and, finally, William.

William looked at Lucy and reassured her. "You will enjoy your salad. It's all fresh and filled with berries and nuts. Plus they make their own dressing."

Abruptly, Lucy said, "I sat in on one of Mary's classes that first week. What I saw was—" She paused, shook her head, and continued, "She had this effect on the students that could be seen in their faces. They wanted to be there. You could tell that by their expressions. It wasn't that they had to be. They wanted to be. I don't think I had ever witnessed that before. It was just so evident to me. Those students were thirsty for what she had to offer and the way she offered it. She was handing them something in a way they needed it to be given to them, in a way they could understand." Lucy shook her head. "The way she talked was captivating. From her very first sentence, she had their attention and kept it the entire hour. I found out later that most of the classes she taught would always fill up first." She took a drink of her water and sat quietly and motionlessly.

Kelly looked at her. "She was a real instructor?"

Lucy smiled at her. "Yes, Kelly, she was."

The intensity of their conversation lightened up a bit as their waitress brought their meals. Between bites, Lucy shared her experiences of teaching at a small private college and how integral Jim's and Mary's assistance was at helping her blend in and begin to develop an understanding of the small town of Canton.

Chapter 23

On the way back home, Maria reminded William he needed to call Devon and possibly plan their breakfast meeting.

"You know, with everything going on, it may be easier if we meet them at the cafe."

"I think you're right. That would be easier. When we get home, I'll call them and make plans for the morning. And because of time restraints with Jim and Lucy, we may only have time for coffee. Or we could just schedule it for next weekend or so."

"That's okay. There will always be another chance."

Chapter 24

Lucy got out of the car, thanked them for their kindness, and walked into the hospital.

She was drained emotionally and physically. Once she finally did sit down to rest, sleep consumed her mind and heart.

Chapter 25

Jim woke up before Lucy. He stared at the emptiness of the room and likened it to what he was experiencing in his life at that moment. *It is empty,* he thought. *It is void of what mattered the most to me for many years. How will I adjust? How will I survive?*

He knew he would because he trusted in Christ. He knew the pain would subside over time, but the loss of Mary would take longer. There would be a gaping hole to fill, but he knew that something would fill it.

Lucy was asleep in the chair with a blanket over her legs.

Just then the door opened, and a nurse walked in as Lucy woke up. The nurse smiled. "Dr. Scott has released you any time you want to leave. He would like you both to join him and his wife for breakfast at their home." She handed them a piece of paper. "Here are the directions. It's easy to find. You may leave anytime you feel ready. There are a few papers to sign as you leave, but that will take only a few minutes."

Jim looked at her. "Thank you very much. Could I also ask whether my wife's body has been picked up for cremation?"

The nurse said, "Yes."

Both Jim and Lucy thanked her for her kindness, and Jim said, "We will be leaving shortly."

Lucy got up from the chair, placed the blanket on it, looked at Jim, and motioned to a bag on the floor. "I took the liberty of bringing in your overnight bag. I'll go get your paperwork while you get dressed."

"Thank you. It won't take me too long. I will meet you at the front desk."

She smiled and started to leave the room, but Jim asked, "Could you stay for just a moment? I need to tell you something."

"Sure."

"When the medics were attending to me at the scene of the wreck, one of them told the other my right hand was clenched. I guess he anticipated an injury of some sort. He asked if I could open it, and I did, but what I saw I did not understand. There, in my palm, rested a dime. I don't remember grabbing it, or if I did, why I would have. It's a mystery to me, but I know it is somehow connected to everything that happened there by that rest area." He looked at Lucy questioningly but said nothing.

She said, "I don't know either, but for a reason I too don't understand, William or Maria may know. We can ask them when we arrive there."

"That's fine. I'll be right out."

He changed and joined Lucy at the front desk to finish up his paperwork. It took only a few minutes, and they were out the door walking to Lucy's car.

As Jim walked out into the morning sun, he paused and viewed their surroundings. He looked at Lucy. "I feel this is so unreal. It's like I expect Mary to be in your car or for her to instantly appear."

Lucy reached over and took hold of his hand as they walked to her car.

At the car, she let go of his hand.

He stopped again. "It just seems like a bad dream." He placed his hands on the top of the car to steady himself as his emotions overcame him. He bowed his head to the pain and sobbed.

Lucy stepped close and placed her hands on his shoulders to comfort him.

For moments that were undefinable by time and space, he would simply exist in that dark space that contained no answers.

He raised his head, looked at her, and simply said, "Let's go."

They both got into her car and left for William and Maria's home. He sat in silence as Lucy followed the directions on the piece of paper. They left the city limits and headed east of town a few miles to a side road.

She looked over at Jim. "This is our turn. The note says it's a quarter of a mile down this road."

Jim just smiled and looked in the direction of Lucy's turn. It was a wooded drive that offered nothing out of the ordinary. The area opened up to a large mowed lawn with a conservative-looking red cedar home. There was a large lake behind the house and woods past that.

Jim spoke first. "This is a comfortable-looking place, isn't it?"

"Yes, it's very pretty here." She looked over at him. "I really didn't expect anything too big. They don't seem to be that type of people."

Jim agreed. "No, I would expect something like this. It's quiet and peaceful here."

She pulled the car up to the parking area in front of the house.

The front door opened; and William, Maria, and Kelly came out.

They walked up to the car, and William spoke first. "Welcome to our home." He smiled at them, and Maria said, "Please come in. Breakfast is ready."

Kelly looked at them. "Do you both drink coffee?"

Jim looked her way. "Yes, thank you." He stopped and looked around the yard and the surroundings. "Mary would have loved seeing this. This would have been just her cup of tea. She had always grown up rural. It gave her a sense of being part of everything. A sense of belonging to something greater than herself."

"Speaking for all of us," William said, "we wish we could have known her."

Kelly stepped up to get the door for them. As they entered, they walked directly into a dining/kitchen area that seemed to be most of the center of the house. When one sat at the table, one could see the lake beyond the windows.

Jim said, "Mary would have loved that view."

The table sat in front of the windows that ran the entire length of the room. The lake could be seen shore to shore.

Jim looked to the left side of the room where an immense fireplace sat and for a moment stood silently.

No one said a word. They knew Jim was wandering through Mary's thoughts or the ones she would have had had she been there.

He pointed to the fireplace. "From a small child Mary's life always contained a fireplace or woodstove. One of our first dates was spent in front of the fireplace that was in her parents' home. She told me that it brought their family together. In the winter, they sat around it and shared their day's experiences. Her parents were an amazing couple. They rarely said anything without thinking. You could see it in their expressions, in the way they held their eyes. They were very dedicated to each and to her. She was their only child." He looked at the set table. "Looks like we're ready to eat."

Maria spoke first. "The hospital called and told us you were on your way. We wanted the food to be hot."

William motioned. "Please sit."

They each moved around the table and took a chair, but before anyone could sit down, William said, "Could we pray first?"

Jim answered, "Please do."

They all bowed their heads, and William offered a short prayer of thanksgiving and healing and then said, "Please sit."

As they were all sitting down, Jim looked at William. "Something happened at the wreck scene that I remembered last night, and I don't know the significance of it." He looked at Lucy and continued, "We both agreed that you may have an answer for us."

"What did you remember?"

Jim related the story of the clenched fist and the dime in his palm. Instantly, Maria looked at William. They all noticed her look, and Lucy was the first to speak.

"Then there is some significance to the dime."

William looked at all of them. "Yes, there is something very powerful about the dime. Many years ago, Maria and I began finding them in the strangest places. It didn't seem to matter where we were at the time. We would notice a dime wherever we might be. The first one we found out there." He pointed through the windows. "We took a walk out to the dock and found one lying there. We just figured that one of us had dropped it. But then we found another one on our way to work. When we got back home that day, we had found at least ten to fifteen in all kinds of places. Extremely curious, we googled the significance of ten in Christianity."

"What did you find?" asked Kelly, for she had not heard this story.

William answered, "It can mean that a new divine order may be coming." He smiled. "Coincidentally, many more things began happening or coming out of Rest Area 10 after the dime experience happened."

Maria added, "There seemed to be a certain flow or movement of happenings surrounding that place and our lives. We began to expect things. We began to anticipate things. Something was happening there. Lives were being touched, and lives were being transformed by Someone that no one expected in a place that doesn't really exist."

Jim, Lucy, and even Kelly, sat transfixed by what Maria was saying.

William noticed their silence. "We never asked Him why these things were happening. We just accepted that they were and that we were supposed to be somehow connected to the ones that came our way."

Jim looked at him. "What do you mean 'came your way'?"

William looked at Maria. "Maria and I both agreed that there may be situations that happened out there that we are unaware of. After all, Rest Area 10 is not always about us. It's about the people that are led there and the reasons they are. We don't determine their comings and goings. We simply offer our support when they do come our way. At times, we indirectly hear of a situation that may have happened there."

Kelly said, "The other night, in the den, when I found your book and read some of your thoughts, I felt as if a portion of them came from or had their beginnings with something connected to Rest Area 10."

William said, "Some of them did, Kelly. I built my thoughts around how I interpreted what I had heard. I wanted to remember what was happening to me and why I believed it was. You see, that small piece of land had become a piece of everyone that had been there or, for that matter, would ever be there."

Jim looked at everyone and interrupted each one's thoughts. "And now we are part of all of this."

William said, "But one thing we all have to remember." He stopped and looked at Jim. "Rest Area 10 does not separate us from each other. It does not leave us alone. It may alter our journeys, but it brings us together. It binds us. If something is taken away from us, there is a reason it has been, and it will be replaced with something else." He smiled at the gathering. "Let's eat before our food gets cold. We don't want the cooks to be mad at us."

They all laughed and began the breakfast.

Chapter 26

The old truck slowed to a stop. The driver looked over at the young man. "Sorry, kid. This is my turnoff. Hope you find whatever it is you're searching for."

The young man got out of the truck, turned, and thanked the man for the ride.

The driver smiled. "You be careful out here on the highway hitchhiking."

"I will. Thanks for the conversation."

As the truck sped off to the south, Jimmy looked down an empty road. He looked up into the sky as if to find an answer. He looked to the direction the truck had gone and then to the north. Thinking to himself, then out loud, "I'm not sure which direction I should go."

He looked up again to an overcast sky. He had no idea what to do at this point. He took his backpack off, unzipped a pocket, and took out a bottle of water. He took a sip from it and decided just to sit before he started walking again. Walking off the roadside a bit, he sat down and took another drink of water. He sighed and spoke to no one again.

"Maybe I made a mistake in leaving, but what other choice did I have? I really didn't leave anything or anyone. I just left where I was at. It was a point that offered me nothing. It was simply a stop in the road. A place to rest. A place to build up the strength and courage to keep moving. Where should I go? If I stand up, which direction should I walk?" He chuckled. "Maybe I'll just flip a coin. Heads, I go west. Tails, I go north."

He reached into his pocket and felt only one coin. He brought it out. It was a dime. He placed it on the nail of his right thumb and flipped it into the air. As it was returning to the ground, he thought, *If it lands heads, I'll go west. If it lands tails, I'll go north.*

It landed heads. He picked it up, stood up, and began walking to the west.

He hadn't gone far when he heard a vehicle approaching from behind him. He turned and stuck his hand out to signify he was hitchhiking.

The car slowed down and stopped. The driver, an elderly man, rolled the window down.

"Need a lift, young man?"

Jimmy answered with a smile. "I sure do."

"Hop in."

Jimmy opened the door and slid inside the car.

The man stuck his hand out. "People call me old Ben Waters, and you are?"

"I'm Jimmy Parker."

"Glad to meet you, Jimmy Parker. Where you headed?"

Jimmy looked out the windshield and pointed. "I'm going that way, I guess."

Old Ben looked at Jimmy. "I'll take you down the road a piece."

"How far you headed?"

He smiled at the young man. "Maybe only as far as you need to go." He smiled at the boy and laughed a little. "Let's get started." He pulled back onto the road and headed west.

Ben looked over at Jimmy. The boy looked tired. “If you’re tired, lean back, close your eyes, and get some sleep.”

Jimmy did not feel threatened at all. In fact, he looked at Ben. “You have kids and grandkids?”

Ben smiled back at Jimmy. “Yes, I have lots of children. We can talk about that later. You get some sleep. You look worn out.”

“Thanks.” He sat back against the seat, closed his eyes, but before sleep overtook him, he thought, *What did Ben mean he was going as far as I needed to go?* He took a shallow breath. No answer came, but sleep did.

Chapter 27

A bump in the road stirred Jimmy from his sleep. He looked over at Ben. The old guy apologized for waking him up. "You slept for over an hour, Jimmy. You must have needed the nap."

Jimmy wiped his eyes and chuckled. "Guess I did."

Ben looked at him. "Tell me a bit about yourself if you don't mind me asking." But before he could start, Ben said, "You look like a clean-cut type of a kid. You're obviously concerned about your appearance."

Before Jimmy said a word, he looked at Ben and thought, *This guy looks like someone's grandpa.* He was neat, nicely dressed, and had a warm expression on his face. Kind of a genuine type person. Someone that he was not used to.

Jimmy began. "Well, I'm eighteen, and I guess I'm out on my own now. Maybe just trying to find where or if I fit in somewhere."

"Do you have a family?"

"No, not really. I was orphaned and never really knew who my mother and father were. I was in foster homes for all of my eighteen years. Some were good, and regrettably, some were not so good." He smiled at Ben. "But that's behind me. As soon as I turned eighteen, I headed out on my own to see what I could find."

"What have you found so far?"

Jimmy laughed. "Not much. I really have only been out on the road for about ten days." He thought for a second and looked at Ben. "But I have a strange feeling that this may be my lucky day."

"What can you do?"

"Well, that's one good thing about a few of the foster homes I was in. I did learn basic skills helping out around the homes I lived in. Most of the husbands were men of trades, like plumbers, carpenters. Guys that knew how to fix things, I guess is what I'm saying."

"That's a good thing. One can always find a job with those kinds of skills and abilities. Did you complete school?"

"I did. I really liked learning things. Maybe because it took me away from my life and somehow allowed me to live in another way. It seemed what I was learning was beyond most of the home situations I was involved in. Maybe I was thirsty for something. Guess I felt empty, and what I learned kind of gave me a full feeling, like I was learning something of value, something I could always use in life."

"What subjects did you like the most?"

"Well, I liked history, but I also liked what I heard in some of the churches I attended with my foster families."

"Like what?"

"Oh, nothing really in particular, but I always wondered about Jesus. I mean about what He must have really been like. Guess I have lots of questions without answers. Even though I went to church, I never really connected with anything there. They just seemed to never really give a good explanation who Christ was. Or maybe who He still is. I'm probably not making any sense, am I?" Jimmy paused and looked over at Ben. "You're obviously retired, but what did you do when you worked?"

Ben smiled and glanced at Jimmy. "I have always been in a profession of helping people find things in life."

"What kinds of things?"

"There are lots of things that people may want in life or think they can't live without. I simply try to point out those things that they need, not just want. A lot of times what you want may never provide what you need."

Jimmy looked at Ben curiously. "I may be totally off base here, but are you a minister? That sounds like a sermon I heard from one of the churches I went to with my foster parents. I didn't get a whole lot from that church or that family for that matter. I just remember a few things that minister said in a couple of his sermons."

Ben smiled. "Then you did learn something. Something stuck with you. One of the greatest tools we can learn in life is how to ask the right questions."

Jimmy looked at him quizzically. "Never thought of it like that. Maybe I did take something with me. Maybe it's still inside me."

Ben looked at him again. "Maybe there's a lot more in you than even you realize."

"Did you have a church? What denomination are you?" asked Jimmy, trying to avoid Ben's last statement.

"Well, I'm not really that kind of a minister."

"What do you mean?"

"Denominations get hung up on things that really don't have anything to do with Christ and His life. I call it denominational dogma. It promotes the financial well-being of the institution, makes the people feel good about their attendance there, but does little to explain Who Christ is."

Confused, Jimmy looked at Ben. "Then how can you be a minister if you disagree with their doctrines?"

"Christ gave us clear instructions on how we should live our lives. Part of that is simply sharing with others Who we believe Christ is and what He can do in our lives."

Jimmy turned in his seat to face Ben. "What do you mean 'what He can do in our lives'?"

"There's a small cafe up the road just a bit. Would you like to grab something to eat?"

"I don't have much money."

"It's my treat."

Just then they came around a sharp curve, and right in front of them was a small restaurant. Jimmy noticed the empty parking lot. "There are no cars here. Maybe we shouldn't stop."

"It's just the time of the day. I have eaten here before. The food is great, and the people are better."

"It's your money."

They pulled into the graveled lot and up to the front door.

"Let's go see what the special is today."

Walking in, they found only two people inside. One was obviously the waitress and the other the cook.

They were both sitting at the bar and turned to see who had come in. Both man and woman had big smiles on their faces.

The woman said, "Why look, dear. It's old Ben Waters. How the heck are you, Ben? You haven't been in for a while. It's good to see you."

Ben smiled. "It's good to see both of you again as well." He looked at Jimmy. "Jimmy Parker, these two are the Browns. They run the best restaurant this side of the divide."

The woman asked, "What can we get you?"

Ben looked at Jimmy and then at the couple. "What's on special?"

The man looked at Jimmy. "What would you like, young man?"

Jimmy looked stunned that someone would ask him what he liked. He paused a bit and sheepishly said, "I would love a hot roast beef sandwich with mashed potatoes and gravy."

"Then that's what's on special today."

As he got up to go back into the kitchen, the woman said, "You look like a young man that would enjoy a piece of blackberry cobbler for dessert." Smiling, she continued, "Maybe with a dip of homemade ice cream on top."

"That sounds perfect."

"You can sit anywhere you like. What to drink?"

Jimmy said, "Could I get a glass of milk?"

"Absolutely. Coming right up. You want coffee and water, Ben?"

"Thank you, yes."

They sat at one of the ten tables. Jimmy noticed the number of tables and that the restaurant didn't have many decorations. He looked around, and before he could say something, Ben began. "Kind of a sparse place, isn't it?"

"I was just thinking the same thing."

"Sometimes, Jimmy, it doesn't take a lot of stuff to create something of real value in an event or experience—or even a life."

"What do you mean?"

"Well, can I use your life as an example?"

"Sure."

"Okay. You told me you bounced around from one foster home to another. I'm sure you may have been hard to handle or understand, and you probably weren't given very much. Maybe a small amount of compassion along the way. Am I right?"

Jimmy pushed back a little mentally. "Maybe."

"You may have even felt neglected at times, but you still were learning who you were or maybe even who you would like to be, where you would like to go in life."

"You're talking about dreams, aren't you? I mean we all have them, but they're just dreams."

"I am. We all have them. See, you did learn something. You learned something about yourself."

Jimmy looked away from Ben as if he were looking off into space or maybe trying to collect his thoughts from their conversation. He looked back at Ben. "Can I ask you a question?"

"Sure. Ask anything you want."

"When I asked you how far you were going, you said just as far as I needed to go. What did you mean by that? How far is that? What direction do I need to be going?"

Ben looked at Jimmy. "It's not really a place of distance but more of a state of mind. Oh, it can be a physical place, but it's more spiritual than anything."

"How long will it take me to get there?"

Ben smiled at Jimmy. "You're very near to understanding just how close you are."

Just then Mrs. Brown brought their meals. Setting them down, she looked at Jimmy. "Pay attention to what Ben tells you. He has some insight into the comings and goings of life. You never know where what he explains to you might lead." She smiled. "If there's anything else you would like, just ask. I'll bring your cobbler over when you finish your meal."

Jimmy looked up at her. "Thank you. And I think you're right about Ben."

Ben looked at Jimmy. "Eat your meal before it gets cold."

But before he took his first bite, Jimmy asked Ben, "How many opportunities do you think are out there for someone like me?"

Ben took a drink of his coffee. "You don't need to think about others. There is only one correct way for you to go. You may have to wait for it to arrive. And at first, its arrival may come unannounced, but there will be something that spurs you to action."

Between bites, Jimmy asked, "What do you mean 'spurs me to action'? How will I recognize it when it happens?"

Jimmy took another bite as Ben started to explain his reasoning. "Do you remember what you felt like when you first left your last foster home? Do you remember what led you to thoughts of leaving?"

Jimmy swallowed his last bite. "Yes, I just felt the time was right." He paused. "Maybe I was being pushed. Maybe a force was leading me away from where I was." He looked at Ben. "You probably think someone was intervening on my behalf, don't you? I'm saying that from memories of ministers that spoke of how God works."

"Jimmy, once you start following those nudges, as I call them, obeying them becomes much easier. Does that make sense to you?"

Jimmy smiled at Ben. "Yes. I guess that's maybe what I have been attempting to do for several years." He looked down at his food and paused. "I don't have anyone else to trust in my life right now except God."

Ben looked at Jimmy. His face became very intense. Jimmy felt as if Ben were looking right into his heart and soul.

Mrs. Brown came back just then with a piece of cobbler and a scoop of ice cream. "Here you go, young man. Enjoy."

Jimmy looked up with a wide smile. "Thank you."

"Dig in," said Ben. "When you finish, there's a place close by that I want to show you. It's what you need right now."

Jimmy finished his cobbler and thanked the Browns for their hospitality, and he and Ben left the restaurant.

As they were getting into Ben's car, Jimmy turned and said, "I think you forgot to pay them for our meal."

Ben simply said, "There was no charge."

"It was free?"

"Yes."

"That was really nice of them."

"Yes, they are a nice couple. I have known them for a very long time."

Ben pulled out onto the highway.

Jimmy turned and looked at Ben. "Do you come this way often?"

Ben Looked at Jimmy. "Yes, I am by this way a lot." He smiled at Jimmy. "It's kind of surprising what one can run across on this highway."

"What do you mean?"

"People are all going somewhere, Jimmy. Many have problems trying to find the road that may get them there. Sometimes they can get sidetracked and take the wrong road."

"What happens then?"

Ben smiled at Jimmy again. "Well, some stop and ask for advice or are given advice from a complete stranger. Others keep wandering and never find their place. You know, Jimmy, there's no reason to wander aimlessly about trying to find something. In many cases, it's right in your midst. It's right where you are. It's right in front of you."

Jimmy looked back at Ben, frustrated. "How are you to know it's there?"

Ben didn't answer.

He looked again into Ben's eyes, and something or someone took hold of him. Something moved inside this eighteen-year-old kid. He looked outside the moving car to the fields going by, to the tall trees with their branches full of leaves. He looked back at Ben, but before Jimmy could say anything, Ben spoke in a commanding but soft and gentle voice.

"Where you think there are no answers, there are. When you think no one is listening, someone always is."

Ben's car started in to a sweeping curve, and Jimmy noticed a rest area just ahead. He looked at it and squinted. He looked over at Ben. "That looks like it's been here a long time."

"It has been here longer than both of our combined ages."

Jimmy laughed. "How old are you, Ben?"

Ben laughed. "Probably older than you think." Ben slowed the car down and put his turn signal on.

Jimmy looked at him in a strangely anxious way.

Ben looked at Jimmy as he was pulling into the rest area. "This is as far as I go."

"What do you mean? I got the impression you were going a lot farther. You told me you would take me as far as I needed to go!"

Ben quietly answered Jimmy's spontaneous outburst. "This is as far as you need to go."

Anxiety spilled out of Jimmy. "But there's nothing here. It's just an old rest area. There's not even a bathroom."

Ben pulled the car up to a concrete barrier, shut it off, and turned to look at Jimmy. "Let's get out and sit on that bench for a bit before I go. There's something I want to tell you."

They got out, walked the few steps to the bench, and sat down.

Ben stretched his legs out a bit and began. "I know you don't see anything here right now. It seems old and vacant of everything you may be used to, but there's more here than you realize. There's no need to be anxious or fearful. As I just told you, you are in the right place for right now. This is a safe place for you. Don't be anxious. Just relax. Something or someone will come along, and your journey will continue."

Jimmy just blurted out, "Can you promise me that?"

Ben looked at Jimmy, reached over, and placed his right hand on Jimmy's left shoulder. "Yes, I promise that from this old place your journey will continue and you will find a road to some of those dreams we were talking about. Just remember. Every time you walk away from something, you are walking toward something else."

The moment Ben's hand touched Jimmy's shoulder, his fear left him. He relaxed at Ben's statement.

With his hand still on Jimmy's shoulder, Ben continued, "Fear cannot find a home in you. You will be fine. You will only need to be in this place long enough to capture two thoughts."

"And what are they?"

"Why you made it this far, and why you are here." Ben took his hand from Jimmy's shoulder and stood up. "I need to get going."

Jimmy stood up, held his right hand out to meet Ben's, and shook it. "I may not understand this, but I do thank you for stopping and bringing me here."

"You are most welcome. Just remember what we talked about. You'll be fine, Jimmy Parker. The ride to your future is almost here."

"I hope you're right."

Jimmy started to ask Ben another question, but Ben looked at him. "The answer to those two questions I mentioned is in front of you."

Ben looked again at Jimmy as he was getting into his car. He started it, began backing away from the curb, and rolled the window down. "I'm never wrong. The dime fell heads up, didn't it?" With that last statement, Ben pulled out to the highway and headed east.

In a lonely rest area, in the middle of nowhere, an eighteen-year-old young man stood motionless. He wanted to respond to Ben. He wanted to ask more questions of the old man, but Ben was gone. Jimmy turned to view his surroundings. He was in an emotional daze. The last few hours seemed like a dream, like it hadn't happened. Jimmy looked around. Then something took hold of him, and he said out loud, "How did he know about the dime?" There was no one there to answer his questions, but he spoke out loud again. "Who are you, Ben Waters?"

He turned and looked both ways. He looked east, and he looked west. No one was there. He turned, walked back to the table, and sat down. Again, he looked in both directions down the highway. He looked up to the overhanging trees. He wanted to speak to Ben again.

The wind picked up a bit and quickly walked through the branches suspended above him, and a few leaves floated to the ground. They did not grasp his attention. They fell unnoticed to his senses.

He hung his head a bit, placed his elbows on his knees, and laid his face in his hands. For a split second, no longer than a moment in time, as quick as a bee sting, he became lost within his emotions.

He closed his eyes to the outside world. His thoughts turned inward. He heard Ben's voice.

"I'm never wrong. The dime fell heads up, didn't it?"

He opened his eyes to the leaves on the ground. Again, a gentle wind moved across his senses, and the leaves on the ground responded. He watched them. He began to see a direction to their movement. They were being placed in a certain position by an unseen hand, and when the wind stopped, he was amazed at what lay upon the ground before him.

The power of the moment took hold of him. On the ground, just beneath him, just beneath his thoughts and his emotions, neatly placed end to end and side to side lay a perfect Cross made of leaves.

I am not alone, he thought.

Chapter 28

Lucy and Jim said their goodbyes to William, Maria, and Kelly; got into Lucy's car; slowly pulled from the driveway; and headed to a future they were unsure of but had faith in.

Jim looked at Lucy. "I am perfect to drive if you want me to."

"I'm okay. Just sit back and relax as best you can. There's a lot ahead of us, more for you than me, but we'll get through it. And who really knows what's around the next curve in the road."

Jim smiled at Lucy, rested his head against the back of his seat, and closed his eyes to what lay in front of them.

Lucy wanted to reassure him but held her thoughts for another time. *It's difficult moving forward from here*, she thought. She asked herself, *How do I look ahead when everything I value in the moment is lost behind me?*

But like the miles in front of them, each day and week would slide by, and each tomorrow would be better than the last. There would be nights that would be consumed by a loneliness that neither of them had ever experienced. There would be cries in the night, but these too she knew would pass.

She knew her focus would change from what she had lost to what Mary meant to her, and for a time, the holes in her emotions would be vacant, but they would once again be filled by something.

Her faith had taught her that. She knew that Christ would never leave her alone.

She smiled and thought, *My life is like a wall with a big hole in it.* The hole was unexpected and had come without notice. It exposed a weakness, a weakness that she did know existed. It was a hole that allowed the cold and darkness of loss to blow in and steal the strength away from her. It was a helpless feeling of aloneness, of being stranded somewhere with no perfect direction to turn, nothing to stop the pain. The hole allowed an emptiness to steal her emotions and raise her doubt in all she believed in. She shook her head, regained her composure, and smiled.

She smiled again at the peace that enveloped the car and thought, *Christ is already patching the hole.* He had started the process of repair, long before the hole had opened up.

She thought of what Jim had seen at the wreck, of what he had heard.

Under her breath and barely a sound, she whispered, "You're always at work. Thank You, Lord. Thank You."

The miles would slip by. Both Lucy and Jim would be consumed by thoughts of the past and prayers for the future. It would be a ride cushioned on the air that would blow in from a place far away yet as close as a prayer.

Lucy looked over at Jim. He slowly opened his eyes. They were filled with tears. He closed them and opened them.

"I just saw Mary. She told me not to worry, for in every curve that we move into, we will always move out of it stronger than we entered." He looked out of the windshield, cried a little, and continued, "It was such a moment of peace. For just an instant, Lucy, I felt no pain, no sense of loss. There was a sense of expectation, a sense that something was on the horizon." He looked over at her questioningly. "I felt like she was imparting a sense on non-concern for today and tomorrow. It was a sense of confidence that slid into me and gathered up my doubt, my anxiety, and pushed it out of me." He paused again and looked out the windshield to the road in front of them and gasped. "Oh, my God. Look!"

Lucy saw it as quickly as he did. "Oh, my Lord. I have chills running through my entire body." She looked at him, grabbed his arm. "We have to stop. We have no choice. It is there for us. We have to stop."

"Absolutely."

She slowed the car down. In front of them, not a quarter of a mile ahead of them, at the curve in the road, sat Rest Area 10 and on a picnic table sat what appeared to them to be a young man.

Chapter 29

As Lucy slowed her car down, the young man sitting on the picnic table looked their way.

Lucy looked over at Jim. He had excitement written all over his face. She smiled at him, and he said, "We both know, don't we, that this young man is here for us?"

"Yes." Lucy smiled.

She pulled the car up to the concrete curb and shut it off, and they both got out.

Working with young kids in a college environment, both were very effective at starting a conversation to make one feel at ease.

Jim looked at the young man. "You know several years ago I was probably doing the same thing you are. I was hitchhiking my way to my future, or so I thought."

To both their surprise, the young man asked, "Did you make it?"

Jim looked at him. "Yes, I did. I might have thought it was kind of a grueling experience back then, but it worked out, and I am doing what I thoroughly enjoy."

"And what is that?"

"I am a college professor." Jim walked a bit closer to the young man, stuck his hand out, and said, "I'm Jim Parker, and this is Lucy Erring."

The young man sat motionless, almost transfixed somewhere in his own thought, and for a split second said nothing.

Lucy asked, "Is there something wrong?"

The young man looked at them and apologized. "I'm sorry. It's just that we have the same name. I'm Jimmy Parker." He stuck his hand out and shook Jim's first, then Lucy's.

"Are you headed in any specific direction?" asked Lucy.

Jimmy smiled. "Well, according to an old man that gave me a ride here. This is where I find my future." He looked away for just an instant. "I have been in and out of foster homes my whole life and never met anyone like this old guy. It has been so strange. Everything today just seemed like it occurred for a reason."

"Maybe it has," answered Jim.

Lucy looked at Jimmy. "Do you mind if we sit down?"

"Not at all. I'm not going anywhere."

As they both sat down, Lucy asked, "Could you tell us about the old man that dropped you off here."

"Sure."

He began explaining to them both about how he had met Ben and the things they had talked about, their lunch together at the old restaurant, and then his dropping him off in this rest area. Jimmy looked from Jim to Lucy.

"I don't think I have ever met anyone like him. He seemed to know more about me than I know about myself. When he dropped me off, talked to me, and then left, I felt as though I had just lost my best friend. I had the strangest feeling." Jimmy raised his eyebrows as if to show surprise or excitement and continued, "I didn't tell you about his last words to me as he left here. Before he came by, I was sitting along the road trying to decide what to do, what direction to go. I took a coin out and told myself if it landed heads I would go west and tails, I would go north. It landed heads, so I started walking to the west. It was after that that Ben came by."

Lucy interrupted Jimmy. "What was the coin?"

"It was a dime."

Jim and Lucy looked at each other, and Jim said, "Please continue, Jimmy."

"Well, we pulled in here and got out. Ben said he wanted to tell me a few things and this was as far as he was going. I was somewhat surprised because he told me earlier that he would take me as far as I needed to go." Jimmy looked at both of them, then out to the highway, and began again. "He reassured me that I did not need to go any farther, that something was on the horizon. It's kind of weird, but for some reason I believed his words."

"What do you mean?" asked Lucy.

"Well, I felt almost betrayed by a man that I had only known for a few hours, but he seemed to know that. He seemed to know exactly what I was thinking, that I was becoming fearful of what would happen next."

"Did he answer those thoughts?" asked Jim.

"Yes, he did. And it was with such confidence that I relaxed in them."

"What did he say?" asked Lucy.

"He told me fear had no place in me, that I would be fine. I asked him if he could promise me that. I asked if he was sure he was right. As he was pulling out of the here, he told me he was never wrong, that I would be fine here, and then said, 'The dime landed heads up, didn't it?'" Jimmy looked at them both again and paused. "He did not pick me up till after I flipped the coin to determine my direction." Jimmy looked at them both again. "How would he know that?"

There was a moment of silence among them. Noticing this, Jimmy asked, "Are you my ride to somewhere? I mean Ben told me that my future was almost here, or something like that. And then not long after that, you came in. I'm not sure what is going on here, but I'm not fearful or scared. He told me that fear had no place here. I feel as though one or both of you may have some answers. Am I just imagining this, or do you know what I'm talking about? Do you know who Ben is?"

Chapter 30

Lucy stood up and looked around Rest Area 10 and then to Jimmy. "You may find this difficult to believe, Jimmy. But today, right now, this place was created for you. What has happened in your life before Ben dropped you off here was so that you may understand this day. Every experience you had in every foster home was preparing you for what is occurring right now, and I'm not sure about this, but I believe that you believe."

Jimmy said nothing but nodded his head in agreement.

She looked at Jim and continued, "We don't know your situation, but we do know that we are part of your future. That's why we are here. That's why this rest area is here. At this moment, this rest area was created just for you. It's a place to get started. It's a place to begin."

Jimmy looked at them both, then around the rest area. He lowered his head as if to look at the ground and saw the leaf Cross. Tears started to build in his eyes as he remembered Ben's words. He looked from Jim to Lucy and pointed to the ground. "I watched that form as I heard his words coming from somewhere, once again telling me I would be fine." Jimmy looked at the Cross of leaves and continued, "I am not scared about where I go from here. I don't think I really ever have been scared, even the day I left the last foster home. There was a sense that faith was leading me." He looked up and straight ahead. There were tears running down his cheeks. "When I would get upset in the whole foster-home situation, I would take a walk. The walk and what I heard inside of me kept giving me a sense of peace. I didn't know what the future would hold for me. But I did, for some reason, know that I would have a future. And that it would be quite different than my foster-home experiences." He paused and looked at them both. "Before today, before my experience with Ben, I felt scattered. I felt as though there were parts of me left in all the foster homes I had lived in and left. I felt disjointed, not whole."

Lucy interrupted. "Do you feel whole now?"

Jimmy looked at her. "I'm not sure if I feel whole, but there is a peace within me, an excitement as I look toward tomorrow that I have never had." He once again looked around Rest Area 10 and then looked at Lucy. "You know who Old Ben is, don't you? I get the feeling you may have even met him before."

Lucy and Jim stood up, looked at each other and then to Jimmy.

Jim began, "Jimmy, we both know who Ben is, and you must trust in why he brought you here. Lucy and I have both had experiences here in Rest Area 10 that have changed the course of our lives. If you want to go back to our college with us, we will explain along the way. We both know, and maybe even you do at this point, that your future lies where we are going, not where you have been. Will you go with us?"

"I don't think I have a choice, at least according to Ben." Jimmy paused and looked around the rest area. "I only knew Ben a few hours, and yet I trust what he said completely. He told me fear had no place in me." With some excitement in his voice, Jimmy said, "I'm ready whenever you are."

"Let's get going then," said a smiling Lucy.

"We'll explain more along the way," said Jim.

They all walked to Lucy's car, got in, and headed east to new futures that were yet to unfold.

Chapter 31

William and Maria left the den to Kelly and her thoughts. They turned as they were walking out and said, "If you need anything tonight, just ask."

Kelly smiled. "Thank you. I will."

As the door closed, Kelly remembered the envelope that contained her dad's and mom's thoughts on life. She got up, looked at the room and the fire, and mentally and emotionally readied herself for what she would read. Unzipping the side pocket on her suitcase, she pulled out the manila envelope. She ran her hands over it. It was well-worn, having been opened many times, she presumed.

She was anxious, but something inside of her drove her anticipation to the top of her emotions. These were thoughts her mom and dad had written just for her. *Were they to be a guide?* she asked herself. Or were they simply her a parents' reflections on life, on how their lives came together, and how they slowly evolved into a marriage that lasted till their deaths? She wondered, *Would these thoughts include tough times or just times full of joy and laughter?*

She looked to the nearby small table and brought a box of Kleenex close. There was no doubt how she might respond reading her parents' thoughts.

She sat in a chair opposite the fireplace, opened the envelope, reached inside, and brought out the contents. The pages were stapled together and appeared probably to be several hundred. They were handwritten. She laughed, knowing that her mom would have written some of them or at least copied what her dad had written. She smiled again, thinking how almost unreadable her dad's penmanship was.

She turned it to see the front. It read, "To our daughter Kelly."

The next page began,

> You were always the most important aspect of our lives. We both always believed that Christ brought us together to have you and raise you in a way that He directed us. We believed that all of what He provided us was to benefit you and the direction you would need to move in life.
>
> We were never very rich, but money was never our focus or our point of concentration.
>
> We can't tell you we were always successful in all of our endeavors, but because of the strength and courage He imparted to us, we were able to provide for you all that was needed to get you where you needed to go.
>
> Somehow, after the events connected to Rest Area 10, there was no doubt Who would guide us and Who was always listening to our thoughts and our desires.
>
> We talked many times of the overall significance of what happened that day at that old rest stop. The events could never be ignored, even in everyday life. It was a bridge from what we understood and where we were to what we hoped for and to where we had hoped to be led.

Christ connected our lives, and Christ created events in our lives that would prove His existence. He became a constant thought in every moment of every day.

And it all started in that little cafe where we were brought together. And it was why we felt compelled to buy it and make it our life's work, at least for that point in our lives. Even when you worked as a waitress as a young teenager, we believed that Christ was guiding you into a process of learning empathy for others, learning to understand a customer's thoughts when they were offered. Neither of us knew where you would go in life, but we both knew beyond any doubt that the cafe was an integral part of your life at that point in your life and it had to occur. We chose paths based on where we thought your direction needed to go.

Our lives may not have been as profound as we might have envisioned them to be, but what we produced through Him would be.

Your mom and I both knew that somewhere on your road in your life all that we brought to you through Him would be manifested in greatness. Not as others may see greatness, but as Christ sees greatness. We somehow knew that our desires in life were not about us but about getting you to a point.

We sincerely believe that He gave us you for reasons we may never realize or be able to experience.

Nonetheless, we knew you were our gift from Him. And we also knew that through Him, we were entrusted to create a foundation upon which your life would be built.

We had times in our lives when our faith was tested. And there were times when we slipped and fell, but He was always was there to pick us up, brush us off, and get us going again.

Right before we encountered Rest Area 10, my faith slipped into a dark place when I thought we were losing you, but thanks to your mother and her strength and her belief in the power of Christ in our lives, she never gave up hope in Him Who created you.

He did not give us a possession in you. He gave us a part of Himself, and the whole time I was racing to get to the next hospital, your mother was reminding Christ of our walk with Him.

As your little head lay on her lap in the back of the car, she kept saying over and over, "He will not let us down. This is His child. He will not let her die. He will not!"

And to strengthen our Faith in Him, our prayers, and our beliefs, He met us at Rest Area 10. He created Rest Area 10 that day for us and you and for whatever He had in store for your life.

It was both of our deeply held beliefs that we might not get to see everything in your life

> come to fruition. But then, it was not necessary for us to. It was only necessary for us to get you to a point where you were no longer simply moving from our teachings but from what had occurred in your life because of our teachings.
>
> And now, as you read our thoughts, you are moving in a new direction.
>
> And as you start to read through them, we both believe that for some reason we know you are there or are close to Rest Area 10. We both know that no matter where you end up, you will always be close to Rest Area 10.

Kelly lay back against the chair, closed her eyes to the beauty of the room, the crackling of the fire, and began remembering her life as her parents had provided and Christ had directed.

Chapter 32

Kelly was still asleep in the chair when William came in and calmly woke her up.

"I don't mean to startle you, but I think Maria may have just suffered a mild stroke. Can you help me get her dressed and into our car and to the ER?"

"Yes." She jumped up to follow William.

"What does she…" She paused, trying to regain her composure. "What are her symptoms?"

William stopped, took a deep breath, and looked right into Kelly's eyes. "She, from my initial thoughts, has had a right-sided hemispheric stroke with some aphasia."

"Does she appear to have any motor skills on her left side? Is her speech gone?"

They resumed their walking.

"Yes, her left arm is unusable, and she cannot speak, but thankfully, her right side did respond."

"How does she seem to be?"

"She woke me up by pushing on me with her right arm. When I turned the light on, I could see the effects of the stroke and started to get a little emotional. She made a motion indicating she wanted to write, so I quickly grabbed a tablet and pen."

"What did she write?"

"She made me promise that in all our conversations about her condition, they would be carried out in front of her. She stressed not to hide anything from her. I promised." William wiped his forehead in exasperation. "In all the years of seeing and working with stroke victims, I never imagined either of us to be in this position."

Kelly grabbed his hand and looked at him with deep, focused concern. "Let's go to her and pray along the way."

William nodded. "Strengthen me, Lord. I need every bit You can give me."

He stopped before going in the bedroom and looked at Kelly. "At this point, all of her cognitive functions are intact. She will know and understand what is going on, but the only way she can respond is writing."

They entered the room just as Kelly repeated William's prayer for strength.

Maria was on the bed and waiting. She handed William the tablet and indicted for him to read it aloud.

He looked at what she had written and read, "Do not hide anything from me. Have all your conversations in front of me. Do what is necessary, but do not do what is unnecessary."

Maria reached up with her right hand, squeezed William's hands, and indicated she wanted to write more.

He handed the tablet back to her, and she wrote more, then handed it back to him.

He read it aloud. "It's okay, dear. We have faced other problems together. We will face this one with the same strength and courage as all the rest. We will not give into fear or desperation. Remember Who we live for and why. There will be a moment when we are allowed to vent our emotions to each other. But right now, let's follow with what our lives have taught us. Right now, let's use our knowledge and experience to cover the necessary bases. Right now, we must be doctors. Then, when that is accomplished, we can immerse ourselves in each other's emotions. We will not waste valuable time in repeatedly asking why this has occurred."

William looked at Maria, then to Kelly. "I agree. I will call Bill Randolf and let him know what's going on and to meet us at the ER." He looked at Kelly. "Bill is our resident neurologist. He can make preparations for all the necessary scans and MRIs. While I call him, can you assist Maria in getting dressed?"

"Yes, absolutely."

As William stepped out to make the call, Kelly looked at Maria, not really knowing what to expect.

But Maria reached out with her right hand to Kelly's arm, gently squeezed it, and smiled a slightly crooked smile as if to reassure her.

Kelly had practiced long enough to know everything would not be fine. This was a debilitating stroke or series of strokes. She silently questioned Maria's behavior. It was difficult for Kelly to accept Maria's calm demeanor.

She squinted her eyes a bit and thought, *I have never seen such resilience in a person, such courage in the face of such odds.*

"Can you point me to where and what clothes you would like to put on?"

Maria pointed her to the walk-in closet, and as Kelly opened the doors, Maria pointed to a top and pair of plain brown pants. While Kelly was getting them ready, Maria was writing once again on the tablet. When she finished, she handed the tablet to Kelly. Kelly looked at it and shook her head. She looked down at Maria. "You are something."

Maria put hand to her mouth and then took it away, indicating she wanted Kelly to read what she had written aloud. Kelly nodded.

"It would seem that a spot in the ER has opened up for you. Maybe in your free time today you can begin making preparations for your move."

Kelly shook her head at what she read and looked at Maria. "How can you be so calm about all of this? How can you be so accepting of what has occurred?" Tears ran from Kelly's eyes and down her cheeks.

Maria reached up with her right hand, grabbed Kelly's, and mouthed silently the word, "Faith." She then picked the tablet up and wrote more.

Kelly read her written words aloud.

"We do not know when things will occur in our lives and may never understand why they do. But for us, for you, William, and me, we know beyond human understanding that they do occur for a reason, and that reason is His alone. It will always be for the greater good of who we are and where we are going. We are temporary, Kelly, but what He has placed inside of us is not. What has happened to me, and indirectly to you and William, is because He has caused it. And it will be for His glory and our benefit. No matter what happens after this moment, remember my words because they come to you from Him. We bear the burdens of our lives, not for the benefit of ourselves but for the benefit of others so they may witness the strength we find in the trust we place in Christ."

At this point, Kelly's face was wet with tears.

Maria motioned for Kelly to step close to her. Kelly reached down and helped Maria to get into a sitting position. Maria took hold of Kelly's arms, pulled her into a tight hug, and held her for a moment.

As she relaxed her grip, Kelly looked into her eyes. "I have never met anyone like you. Your courage and faith are beyond me and beyond human reason. The power He gives you is beyond the measure of man."

Maria looked at Kelly, smiled, and motioned for Kelly to help her get dressed.

It took only a few minutes to get Maria ready to go. As they were finishing, William came back into the room.

"Bill will meet us at the ER, and everything will be ready. I gave him your instructions about being kept in the loop about his thoughts as we progress along through your scans. He agreed. Now let's get some arms under you and get you to the car."

It didn't take them long to get Maria into the car and on the road to the hospital.

William noticed Maria writing on her tablet most of the way there.

As they arrived and pulled up to the very familiar ER entrance, William started to get out but Maria reached up as if to say, "Wait." She handed the tablet to him and motioned to read it aloud.

"Run all the tests that we know are necessary, but when we finish, I want to go home. If something else is supposed to happen, I want to be home. Home is the place we share. It's a place in our hearts, and I want to be there. Promise me that."

He looked at her and then to Kelly in the back seat. "I promise." He reached over and kissed her. "Let's get you inside. The quicker we get the preliminary test and scans done, the quicker we get home."

Chapter 33

The ride back to their home was one of silence. William drove with his left hand and held Maria's right hand with his right hand. It was not necessary to exchange words. Both knew what the other was thinking. Their thoughts flowed from her heart to his and from his to hers on an uninterrupted highway with more emotions than could ever be put into words. These were thoughts that came and went and left something inside each of them for the other. These were thoughts that fed the soul of the other.

At this moment, each of their lives could not be fuller, could not have more meaning, could not have more understanding and compassion. At this moment, their lives moved far beyond the physical sense of living and loving. At this exact moment, Christ gathered them up and eternally placed them together to encounter whatever lay ahead of them, not in fear of the unknown but in joy of the unexpected.

William pulled into the driveway and up to the front door. He let go of Maria's hand. "We'll get you out and into the wheelchair." He looked at Maria. "Is there any place you would like to go to right now?"

She grabbed the tablet on her lap and wrote. "Please take me to the den so I can look out at the lake. I know we don't need a fire, but could you build a small one, please?"

"Absolutely."

From the back seat Kelly said, "I'll step out and get the chair ready."

William and Kelly worked in unison to get Maria out of the car and into the wheelchair.

Kelly looked over at William. "I'll push Maria into the house if you would like to get the door."

"That's fine."

With little effort they got her into the house and then to the den.

Maria pointed to a place by the window.

Kelly got her into position. "Would you like me to get anything for you?"

She looked up at Kelly with that crooked, understanding smile, then looked down at her tablet, and wrote, "William's book please."

As William was building the fire, Kelly quickly got his book as Maria continued writing. She handed the book to Maria as Maria handed her the tablet and motioned her to read it aloud.

"You need to prepare for your trip back home as soon as possible and then for your trip back here. At any point you need William's help, just ask him. We all know everything that has occurred was planned. Christ has created this road for you, and you need to get started on it."

Kelly bent down and kissed Maria on the cheek. "You're right. I'll go get started." She looked at William and walked out of the den.

Chapter 34

With the book lying on her lap, Maria thumbed through the pages. She was obviously looking for something. Maybe it was something that would explain her thoughts, or maybe it was something that would answer the many questions flying through William's mind and heart at this moment. It would satisfy whatever their needs would be.

Whatever it was, it would be appropriate for what lay between just these two people in this quiet place, this perfect room built for their solitude.

She stopped turning the pages and looked at William. She pointed to the words that lay beneath her fingers. They had been ingrained in her psyche from the first moment he had written them when she read them so many years before. She mouthed, "Please read."

William had finished with the fire, and it was crackling. He reached for a chair, pulled it close to Maria, and took the book; but before he started reading, he looked at her. "How do you reach inside yourself and pull something out that is specifically for me, that satisfies a need within me?"

She looked up at him, back to her tablet, and wrote, "The answer lies in the reason I started looking. It is for you and because I knew you needed it to be found and shared. Love will always produce an answer."

He looked at her and silently mouthed, "I love you," and began reading.

> This has never been about the length of our walk together. It's never been about where we have been or where we wanted to go or even what we would gather up along the way. It's never been about a physical place, a place that we could build with what we have made. It has always been about building it with what Christ gave us.
>
> We have worked for it, and maybe we have earned it to some extent from our long labors.
>
> But we both have known that the many gifts we received only reinforced our belief in why we received them.
>
> It's been about all those intangible moments that our two spirits encountered as we moved along this physical plane. It has not mattered if they were not all as we expected them to be or we thought they could be. It only mattered that Christ gave them to us as us! This is how we have moved through His universe. It has always been a flowing experiment about the beauty that was ours as Christ provided as we walked with Him.

She looked at him as tears ran down his face. She reached for his hand. He grabbed hers, and their emotions filled their hearts and ran from one to the other. He pulled closer and tighter to her. It felt as if each needed to be physically and emotionally part of the other. They moved together, their thoughts connected as were their spirits. They understood what each felt about the day, what was happening, and what could happen.

This moment was all that mattered. The one in back of this one was gone. The one in front of this one might never arrive. This one would allow them to capture all that they were supposed to enjoy and all they were supposed to understand.

This was the moment she had talked about earlier. This was the moment when all their emotional protections that had been constructed over so many years helping and healing people were allowed to dissolve and evaporate into what mattered most in their lives—each other!

The only other outside force here would be Christ, but He did not live outside them. He was part of them, part of their thoughts, their actions, and their love. He brought love to them, delivered it Himself, and strengthened it in their life together. This was the foundation He created in everyone's life that encountered Rest Area 10.

After many minutes had gone by and the emphasis each placed on the other was fully ingrained in the atmosphere that settled across this room, they relaxed.

Maria looked at William, pointed to his book, and mouthed, "Please read to me."

William picked the book off the floor where it had fallen because of their embrace and began reading.

It didn't matter to Maria where in it he read or what he read. It only mattered that he read to her. She had to hear his voice. She had to hear his words.

This was how he confronted his world, a world that was hers, a world that made sense to them both, a world that fed the unknown appetite of both.

At this time, this was the best medicine that he could ever administer to her. His voice reached inside of her, carrying every thought that produced every word.

But before he started, he looked at her, looked into her. "How do you reach inside yourself and pull something out that is specifically for me, that satisfies a need within me?" He handed her the tablet.

She wrote and handed it back.

Again, he read aloud, "The answer lies in the reason I started looking, and the answer is it's for you and because I needed to find it for you. I didn't have to look far. I simply had to have the desire to look."

She looked at him, and as he looked at her, she looked deeper than his eyes and wrote more.

He read them.

"My words, just like yours, were meant to bring something alive in you as yours did in me. We have moved together for years as husband and wife, as partners on this planet, but our relationship began not because of William and Maria. It began because of who we are in Christ. We found in each other more than William and Maria. We found a source of strength, of courage, and a strong desire to be who we knew we should be through Him."

William reached over and kissed her. "Thank you."

As they watched the afternoon sun beyond the lake, whatever unknowns that could have been part of their thoughts were consumed by the stillness of what he read and how it he read it.

She was at peace. They were at peace. And faith provided the road to get there.

She looked out the windows to the lake, back to William, and wrote, "What I have lost, we both know will not come back. We must adjust our lives and accept that this may be our future for right now."

Chapter 35

Kelly left Maria, and William and walked to the kitchen. She sat in a chair at the table, placed her elbows on it, and, with her face in her hands, cried.

As a doctor, she understood what had happened and how this might all end.

But now she must decide what she must do and how to do it to benefit everyone involved. She would have to make calls, and there would be explanations that others must hear and understand.

But she knew without a doubt that the road that lay ahead of her was already waiting for her travels. Her only job at this point was simply finding an acceptable way of getting there.

Because it would bring her back here.

She leaned against the back of the seat, closed her eyes, and thought. This was not what she had expected to occur when she had made plans to come here, but it had been a trip that could not be avoided. She was pulled and pushed to return. It never entered her mind not to come back.

She remembered her father's words of how Christ would always direct her life. This was simply one more direction of guidance. It was one that she would eagerly immerse herself into.

However, realistically it was a path of pain. She silently allowed her thoughts to visit the heart of Christ.

She prayed, "Lord, I have fallen in love with these people. I know it's only been a short moment in time as time goes, but through You, their hearts and mine flowed perfectly together. As Mom said many times, 'Thank You, Lord, for being more than I can ever imagine or comprehend.'"

She began making all the necessary calls to the people that must be spoken to. With some regret, she would end her current employment and all the relationships that began because of that job. Ending it would produce a level of sadness.

But with faith decisions would be much easier for her. The beginnings that lay here, the experience of Rest Area 10 unknowingly at her young age, laid all the groundwork that she would ever need to overcome anything in her future.

It took only an hour or so to make preparations for the move and how to make it. She was surprised how it all quickly evolved, but when she finally hung the phone up from the final call, she knew Who was paving the road in front of her.

She laughed to herself and thought, *There may be bumps along the way, but He will even them all out before I ever encounter them or before they can ever exact a toll on me.*

This was supposed to happen.

The little girl that lay critically ill in her mother's lap was supposed to come here, and when time was on her side, she would return.

She shook her head slightly, exhaled, and sat back again in her chair to relax.

She thought about William and Maria and what must be going on in the den. She would not intrude. When he could, William would come out to get her.

Her mind wandered to one thing she had read in her parents' notes to her. They had told her that if she would allow Christ to control her life's wheel, the direction and movement would be at His discretion. It is her wheel, and the trip it takes after all the spokes are in place may not be a long one, but it is the only one that will take her to where she must go. There would be bumps, and there would be mud to overcome, but the same force that turned the wheel allowed it to overcome what lay ahead.

They told her that faith was the energy that causes all things to happen, and they would all be good and for the right reasons.

She relaxed in those thoughts. And at a point unknown to her, she gently slipped into sleep.

Chapter 36

Kelly was still sitting at the table but half-awake when William walked in. She looked at him. "How is she?"

He pulled a chair out and sat down. Leaning against the back, he closed his eyes for a moment and sighed. He opened them up to Kelly. "She is more concerned with you and the transition you need to make to get back here, but I did move her to the couch, and she is resting." He placed his elbows on the table, laid his chin on his hands, and continued, "It's easy to make sense of a situation that requires little strength and faith to understand, but where she finds such faith in this moment is beyond human thoughts. My words cannot define or explain her."

Kelly broke the intensity. "I will start back first thing in the morning and prayerfully only be gone a few days. I made several phone calls, and things surprisingly fell into place after I described the situation here."

William sighed again. "I will take care of everything on this end. The administrators here will more than understand our predicament and will quickly move to get contracts written and ready for your return." He smiled at her. "I don't foresee any problem at all." He looked around the kitchen in a daze and looked back at Kelly. "I was not ready for this, Kelly. I will need your prayers." He smiled at her. "Before you go to bed, Maria would like for you to stop in for a bit."

"I'll go now."

Kelly got up and slowly walked to the den, trying to gather her thoughts along the way. What could she say? What should she do? She may have been trained how to confront these types of physical issues and the resulting emotional responses, but when it happened to you, you're not ready. There's nothing that has prepared you for it. It attacks you, and there's only one way to survive. You pray.

Kelly bowed her head as she walked and simply asked Christ for peace. She stopped, bowed her head once more, raised it, and looked down the unlit hallway that led to William and Maria's bedroom.

Was she expecting to see a response to her prayers? She looked into the hallway again, into the walls, and through the open door that led to the bedroom.

A wind-like movement approached from the room, beyond the door.

She closed her eyes, then opened them, and saw a room that was not filled with furniture but one that was consumed with light. The light moved out of the room, down the hallway, and to her. It softly swirled around her, gathering up all her emotions of inadequacy, and in its place left courage, understanding, and compassion.

And as it moved away from her, she spoke to it. "Thank You. I am ready."

She entered the den. Maria was propped up against the back of the couch so she could view the lake and woods beyond the windows.

As Kelly walked around the couch, Maria took her right arm and patted the cushion of the couch, indicating for Kelly to please sit beside her.

Kelly reached out and picked up both of Maria's hands, held them tightly, and looked into her eyes. Maria moved her eyes to her tablet on the side of the couch as if to tell Kelly to get it.

She let go of Maria's hands and picked the tablet up.

Maria motioned to please read.

Kelly began, "My world as it is may be ending as we know it, but yours is just beginning. He has given you a new walk, a new journey. Without what has happened to me, you would not be coming back here. The creation of this began many, many years ago. It began when you were a small child. It began with your first visit to Rest Area 10.

"Christ is at work here. We cannot allow our sadness to overtake the joy we should feel at knowing that He has chosen us, that He placed us here long before we knew we were coming.

"And, Kelly, it is a beautiful experience. What just happened to you in the hallway will continue to happen along your journey. Your prayers will always be answered the way they need to be to give you strength and understanding."

Kelly stopped reading. She couldn't read any more. Her thoughts filled her eyes. She placed the tablet down, got on her knees beside the couch, close to Maria, and wrapped her arms around her.

She knew she didn't need to find any words at this moment.

At this moment, they were not alone. This was not a moment of pain or sadness. This was a moment when both were wrapped in Christ and the immeasurable power of His love filled their hearts.

Their embrace lasted a few minutes, and each drew strength from the other.

They relaxed, and Kelly sat on the floor beside the couch.

William came in just then and smiled. "I am going to prepare bowls of fruit for Maria and me. Would you like one?"

"Yes."

She looked down at Maria, smiled, and left for the kitchen.

William walked around the couch and told Maria he would bring theirs in and they would eat together.

Maria smiled and nodded.

"I'll be right back."

When William entered the kitchen, Kelly had already begun cutting up fruit for all of them.

She looked his way. "I think I'll take mine to the bedroom and get my things ready for an early morning departure. The quicker I get back home and get things settled, the sooner I will be able to assume my new position."

He walked up to her and gave her a hug. "Thank you."

They finished filling the bowls with fruit, and Kelly left for the bedroom.

She knew what the next few days would be like and wanted to mentally prepare herself for what lay ahead. A simple meal of fruit and a good night's sleep would be her first step.

Chapter 37

William finished the bowls and with bottled water in hand carried it all back into the den.

Maria looked up, smiled a little, and pointed to her tablet. She mouthed to him with silent lips, "Please read."

"Neither of us knows what the next moment will bring. I am not aware of my future, and neither are you. But we are aware that these moments are for the three of us, and we will make use of them with His help."

He looked at her. "That's the only way, dear." He paused. "Now let's try eating and drinking as much as you can."

He would feed her, and their evening would turn into night. With changing clothes and solid hearts, they would work together.

Chapter 38

Today turned into tomorrow, and this week turned into next week. It didn't seem to them that a month or so had passed. They had established a routine that fit everyone's expectations and needs.

Kelly had returned and assumed her new role in the ER. William joined her from time to time, but his main focus was no longer the ER. His passion had been there at one time, but it had been a passion shared by both him and Maria. It was their life's work.

But now their life's work would be each other. It was not one of his taking care of her needs, feeding, bathing, and providing whatever she required; it was one of shared responsibilities. It was a working union that met each one's needs by the other. Maria's disability would not interrupt how she would respond to William. What lay ahead of them was new territory, and they explored it the only way they could—together.

Chapter 39

William and Maria woke up almost at the exact moment. He looked at her, brushed the hair from her face, bent down, and kissed her. He stroked her forehead gently and softly with the side of his hand. She blinked her eyes at him as if to tell him how good it felt. She reached down, grabbed his free hand with her functioning right hand, brought it to her face, and kissed it.

He looked into her eyes. "I could never have envisioned my life like it turned out. When I first pulled into Rest Area 10, I had no idea at all what would transpire over the next forty or so years. It was a dream that actually came to life. We were not simply doctors. We became healers. He led us into a world of sights and sounds and some of the most intimate emotions connected to living and dying that either of us had ever experienced or would ever hope to experience. It was not always easy. It was not always about the living. At times it was about dying, but it was always about understanding life and always in a way He wanted us to.

"At the moment we met each other in Rest Area 10, He knew what would happen. He created each of us for the other and us for others. "He was creating a giant web that would reach out and touch many lives over a wide area. And always at the center of that web, Christ lived and worked through us. It was never about us. It was always about who He could reach through us." He reached down again and wiped her hair away from her face. "Our lives have taught us so many lessons, my dear."

She smiled.

William would have loved to hear her silent voice. Her words had always taught him something or added to the strength of his heart strings. Her words had always bound him to his faith. He thought as he looked at her, *What more could I have ever asked for in my life than to have lived it with someone who understood my life better than I, who understood me better than I did?*

Her eyes met his, and an unspoken language took hold of him. A small tear ran from his face, but before it could run too far, before the meaning of that one tear could escape, Maria raised her good arm and took one small finger and swiped the tear up and touched it to her lips.

It was such a moving moment for William. He wanted to cry but knew Maria had taught him that this was not the end to their lives. It was just another journey, and he knew it would take them somewhere together, as all of their journeys had done. Christ had never left them alone, never by themselves.

He looked at her and, as their day always started because of her stroke, said, "Let me get you to your chair and the windows. Then I will get our tea and oatmeal."

She looked into his eyes and to his heart, smiled, and offered a small wink from her good eye.

He gently lifted her up, placed her in her wheelchair, and pushed her to the windows.

She had always taken her tea by these windows, watching the lake just outside and through the trees.

It was always a place where nature came to life for her. A place of enjoyment. It didn't matter if it was spring and the water was warm with rising fish ready to catch a bug or if it was frozen with a wandering fox or coyote trying to find a meal. It calmed her. It talked to her. This had been her home. She had come here with a man that was more than a mate. Their life was balanced. Their life had moved through many valleys and had risen to many peaks. And yet Christ bound them to each other through His shared Word and His love. Even in their darkest moments when discouragement could have consumed them, Christ continually gave the one strength to give to the other. It was a life of support.

She hadn't sat alone for long when William came back in with her tea and oatmeal. He sat down beside her, and as had happened over several weeks now, he began feeding her. She would raise the teacup with her good hand, take a sip, and look toward William for more oatmeal. She would always smile and wink with the functioning part of her face and good eye.

As they finished their tea and oatmeal, William placed his hand on her arm. "What would you like to do today?" He looked at her, and she looked through the windows and beyond. "Let's take a drive somewhere," he said.

Maria took a drink of hot tea, looked beyond the trees, and then back to William. She paused as if she were looking into something she couldn't see or as if to bring something into focus, into view. She tried to speak but couldn't.

William looked at her, knowing her exasperation at losing her voice, bowed his head, and prayed aloud.

"Please, Lord, give her just one more chance to voice a thought."

She raised her head from his prayer, opened her mouth, and clearly said, "Let's go to Rest Area 10."

What He has given to me, what I have found in life, is only as important as my knowledge that it is because of Him that I have it and because of Him that I must use it.

—Dr. William Scott

About the Author

Ron is a successful rancher/writer. He is intensively involved in his ranch and writing about the benefits of regenerative cattle production in a pasture ecosystem environment. He has written several articles successfully opposing congressional legislation that would have negatively impacted profitability and compromised the integrity of the industry as a whole. He has also shared his beliefs in public forums.

He began writing in college at the suggestion of an English professor who saw raw talent in what he wanted to say but lacked the knowledge and ability to communicate it successfully.

With a determined spirit and a phenomenal relationship with Jesus Christ, doors began opening and opportunities to write a series of books beginning with *Rest Area 10* began developing.